Trade Paperback
ISBN: 1-56315-166-9
© Copyright 1999 Alexander LaPerchia
All rights reserved
First Printing—1999
Library of Congress # 98-87018

Request for information should be addressed to:

SterlingHouse Publisher, Inc.
The Sterling Building
440 Friday Road
Department T-101
Pittsburgh, PA 15209

Cover Art: Michelle Vennare - SterlingHouse Publisher
Typesetting: Pam Muzoleski

This publication includes images from Corel Draw 8 which are protected by the copyright laws of the U.S., Canada and elsewhere.

Printed in Canada

SATAN AND THE SAINT

by Alexander LaPerchia

Forward

People of all faiths can take heart in reading the life of Saint John Vianney who fought Satan and evil for over thirty years. His life is proof that if we love God and conform our lives to His will--we too can be triumphant. It is imperative that people of faith unite now, in combating the darkness which has become so pervasive in our world today. Through obedience to God, prayer and working together we will be victorious over the such evils as the dissolution of families through divorce, the widespread erosion of values and morals, the horror of abortion, the scourge of drug abuse, the escalation of crime, the glorification of pornog[raghy] and violence.

Saint John Vianney withstood the devil's temptations and attacks through his love of God and fellow man. He personified the gospel message of doing spiritual and corporal works of mercy. His life was a triumph of love and goodness. Through this book people of all faiths will be uplifted by the life of this wonderful Saint and see the revelance of his teachings to their own lives. The ecumenical Pope John Paul II honored Saint John Vianney in his speech to priests, deacons and seminarians at a retreat given at Ars on October 6th, 1986. It is a singular blessing that this volume contains his inspiring address.

Dr. Ralph Reed
Executive Director of the Christian Coalation

PART ONE

The Life of Saint John Vianney

"And I will raise me up a faithful priest, who shall do according to my heart, and my soul, and I will build him a faithful house, and he shall walk all days before my anointed." I Samuel 2:35

CHAPTER ONE

Seeds of a Vocation

Are you fed up? With the spate of movies, plays, books, etc. depicting dissolute priests. Don't you think it is high time to read a book that defends the church from all this Catholic bashing? This is that book.

I have written this book because the overwhelming majority of our religious, priests, deacons, brothers, and sisters, deserve as much. Come to think of it, the Catholic laity, myself included, need to rally in support of our church. When I say "our church" I mean just that. We are the Body of Christ, religious and lay. It is we who are under unrelenting attack by the secular media.

Jesus said that his disciples would be persecuted by the world; this sorry truth has never been more glaring than in the diatribes of our critics and enemies today. My purpose in this polemic is to refute them. We can be proud of our Catholic heritage, traditions, schools, hospitals, orphanages, social services. We should not be ashamed of our past nor of who we are. No, we are not perfect. We have made mistakes. What group of people or institution hasn't? We regret failures and offenses of the past. Nonetheless, the good the church has done in the past and present far outweighs its shortcomings.

I trust this brief defense will serve as a cogent

balance for all the unjust negative treatment we have been subjected to.

My approach is two-fold. First, I will examine the life of Saint Jean-Marie Baptiste Vianney, also known as the Cure of Ars. Why this man was canonized and then proclaimed the patron saint of all parish priests will become evident to the reader from this biography. My source materials are the official church records used in the process of canonization. Alas, a series of events this past century has shaken the belief in many people of the spiritual ascent of mankind. Although our Savior has redeemed the world from the grips of Satan, sin still abounds. The evidence is all around us and within us. The role of organized religion as a spiritualizing and socializing agent has generally diminished. Two world wars, the Holocaust, the abomination of abortion, Communism and other forms of dictatorship, soaring crime rates, and the scourge of drug abuse throughout the world, the widespread decline of traditional values, and family life, are horrors that can undermine a person's confidence in man's spiritual progress. Nonetheless, God has always raised up holy people to help us on our journey, to be a beacon of light and hope for us to follow. These souls are the saints, past and present, of all religious persuasions. They burn with a love of God and fellow man. The saint I present to you is an exemplar of holiness for all people, not just our priests. But since John Vianney was called by God to be one of His beloved priests, his life and work is addressed in particular to our clergy. May his life, a triumph of love and goodness over the Evil One and sin, always be an inspiration to priest and layman alike. Hence, my first purpose in writing this thumbnail sketch of Saint Vianney is to uplift and encourage the reader to seek holiness; we will not all be canonized as saints, but, to get to heaven, we must become saints.

My second goal is to have Saint Vianney speak to today's church as he was intimately bound to us in our life's work and mission. The life of a Christian today has never been more difficult. To attain personal sanctification and help others to do so has never been easy, but with God's grace it is always possible. However, the modern lay person, let alone priest, is facing moral obstacles and hardships unimaginable a hundred years ago. It is incontrovertible that we are confronted with massive global decadence and corruption. There has always been iniquity and perversion. But the magnitude and pervasiveness of grievous wrongdoing makes one shudder. Nothing is sacred and no one is spared. All children today are being denied their innocence and tempted to sin; a multitude are being physically, psychologically, and sexually abused. We adults, all of us, through commission or omission stand accused, and the verdict is guilty. Our rampant lack of morality militates against being holy or even good. Truly, this is Satan's century. To lead a Christian life today requires courage, fortitude and indomitable faith. To be a worthy priest is a formidable challenge. Yet this is Christ's charge for all of us; to be deserving of, and made perfect for, God's company in heaven. He has given us saints to aid us on our perilous journey through the tempests of this life to our glorious destination of heaven. They will lead the way in this life and intercede for us when they are in heaven. On the road to his assignment as parish priest of Ars, Saint Vianney received directions from a young boy, Antione Givre, the first parishioner he met on the way to town. He told the lad, "You have shown me the way to Ars, I will show you the way to heaven."

*Abbe Francis Trochu, <u>The Cure of Ars</u>, (Tan Books and Publishers, Rockford, Illinois 1977) p.107. Let us return now to the subject of our attention and inspiration, our estimable Saint John Vianney.

There are multiple determinants which shape the course of a person's life; the personal history of Jean Marie is no exception. We can understand a person's character and personality by knowing his environment, circumstances, influences, etc. from early on. We can only assess a person's development emotionally, intellectually and spiritually by knowing his personal history. The behavior of people is not determined entirely by external stimuli. I do not underestimate the role of reason and conscience inherent in a individual's actions. Nonetheless, our minds are molded to a great extent by others during the formative years. If the experiences are happy ones, we are beneficiaries and tend to become benefactors later on. On the other hand, if our childhood memories are harmful, we have been victims and modern research indicates that those abused tend to abuse. Forgive this digression, but it is important to bear in mind that there are always reasons for a person's outlook and deportment. Love begets love while hatred precipitates strife. This cause-and-effect relationship may appear simplistic, but there is a considerable element of truth to it.

Like that of so many other saints, the provenance of John Vianney was poor and filled with love. He was born on May 8th, 1786 in the country village of Dardilly. His parents, Matthew and Marie, were simple farmers and deeply religious. Jean Marie had five siblings, all dedicated to the Blessed Mother by his mother. Although the town enjoyed peace, France was soon to be ravaged by the French Revolution and infamous Reign of Terror. This was an era of horrific suffering for the populace, a time of deprivation, destruction, and death. People lived in terror, especially in the cities where the guillotine's work never ceased. The "enlightened" leaders of the revolution targeted the intelligentsia and wealthy for imprisonment and execution. The nobility and clergy were held responsible for the oppression of the peasants. Noblemen caused the abject poverty of the peasants; the church blessed their enterprise. Anyone who was educated or monied was suspect. Since the clergy had both, they were reviled and impugned. In retrospect we can judge many of the nobility to be unjust and even cruel to their subjects, but to eradicate all the nobles, including the decent ones, was reprehensible. Class cleansing, like the ethnic cleansing of today, was enforced without mercy. Priests and religious suffered a similar fate. In fact there was a price on the head of every priest. Churches were closed and church land confiscated. The peasants were forbidden to practice religion: celebration of, and attendance at, Holy Mass was a crime, and private donations were frowned upon.

In this poisoned atmosphere it is no wonder that a mood of anticlericalism set in over France. Some common people turned against religion while others became lax in keeping their faith. Others, however, lamented the loss of their priests and nuns, and continued to attend forbidden masses in private homes, even barns, conducted by hunted priests. Their Catholic faith never wavered but grew stronger. Such was the faith of the Vianney family. They could never be convinced that religion was mere hocus-pocus expressed by fools. Nor did they believe that the extermination of the clergy was for the common good. One incident that betokens the fervor of their Catholic faith in the Vianney household took place prior to

Jean Marie's birth. In July, 1770, his grandfather, Pierre Vianney, welcomed a mendicant monk into his home to share a meal. Pierre was a generous man who often hosted the destitute. Jean Marie's father, Matthew, never tired of telling his own children this story as an illustration of Christian cordiality. As it turned out, the wayfaring monk became Saint Joseph Benedict Labre.

Matthew and Marie instilled in their six children love of God and fellow man. They taught their children the instruction of Jesus recorded in the gospels: *"For I was hungry and you gave me food, I was thirsty and you gave me drink. I was a stranger and you welcomed me."* (Matthew 25; verse 35). These words are fulfilled in corporal works of mercy.

Marie Vianney taught her children to pray the rosary. Early on, Jean Marie evinced a great attachment to the rosary. When he was four years old there was an incident he would never forget. His baby sister, Marguerite, desired his rosary beads. She made a fuss, starting to wail. His mother asked him to surrender them to his younger sister. Jean Marie at once gave her the beads although this distressed him greatly. He went but did not utter a word of protest. For his prompt obedience Jean Marie received a small wooden statue of the Blessed Mother. Seventy years later he revealed that he never parted with that statue which he placed beside his bed. He professed a keen love and devotion to the Blessed Mother. In addition, he developed a strong desire to read the Bible. His parents read the Bible to their children; sometimes Jean Marie would kneel on the floor with his hands folded during these sessions.

Of all the children, Jean Marie was the most devout. Although he never bore an air of piety to impress others, his desire to draw close to God did not go unnoticed. When Jean Marie would shepherd a flock of sheep, he would seize the opportunity to construct a makeshift shrine in which to ensconce his statue of the Blessed Virgin. Then he would summon the other children tending their flocks to conduct sermons. He exhorted them to respect their parents, keep good deportment, and love the good God with all their hearts. He loved to lead the children in reciting the rosary and singing hymns.

As a teenager, Jean Marie was not physically imposing. He had brown hair and blue eyes; he was rather short and frail. His angular face was not ruddy, but pallid. Never did he manifest vanity or self-indulgence. Jean Marie contented himself with matters spiritual not material. Years later he revealed that he knew nothing of evil until he learned of it as a priest in the confessional. Jean Marie surmised that his vocation was to be a priest at a tender age. He did not take an interest in girls with the onset of puberty. There was an incident that settled the matter forever. On his way by donkey delivering some corn to be sold, a girl from the neighborhood accompanied him. After a while they sought to rest under a shady tree by the side of the road. No doubt Marian Vincent was fond of Jean Marie. Who would not like a young man who would save up bread and distribute it to other poor families? Marian Vincent used the respite to propose to him. Assuming her parents permission, she offered her heart to him in marriage. Jean Marie was taken by surprise and didn't know what to say. He formulated his response gently but resolutely; his vocation was to be a priest. Sixty years later Marian Vincent recollected the scene with restrained emotion. She accepted his aspiration with a sad heart. From that time on Jean Marie never showed amorous feelings for the opposite sex. Jean Marie received his first Holy Communion surreptitiously when he was thirteen years old. Since public worship was forbidden, the joyous event took place in the private home of Madame de Pingon. There an outlaw priest offered the mass and administered the sacrament of Holy Communion to fifteen children. Jean Marie's sister, Marguerite, the one who had taken possession of his rosary in their infancy, recalled the scene. Her brother was so exhilarated that he did not want to go home. At this time he was given a rosary which he treasured all his life.

With a swiftness to parallel the collapse of atheistic Communism, the Reign of Terror and persecution of the Catholic Church came to an abrupt halt. The First Consul signed a concordat with the Pope re-establishing the Catholic church in France. This was compassed in no small measure through the patient prayers of many of the faithful and exemplified by the Vianney family. On Easter Sunday, April 18th, 1802, the huge bell of Notre Dame pealed the emancipation in Paris. Soon the propitious news reached the town of Dadilly. When Jean Marie heard, he wept unabashedly, declaring to his family his intention to become a priest. He felt that as a priest he could gain many souls for Christ, a prophecy of resounding truth! His family concurred with their blessings.

Jean Marie was nineteen years old when he left his family to enter the newly opened seminary, actually a small rectory school, in the nearby town of Ecully. Jean Marie had to face a trying academic future. Since he had labored on his father's farm all his life, there was little time for study. His elementary studies were deficient, especially the grammar of his native French. When he arrived at the seminary he was greeted by his mentor, Father Balley. This priest presented a stern appearance but had a soft spot in his heart for

Jean Marie. The austere priest practiced what he preached; he prayed intensely, did much penance, and undertook rigorous fasts. Yet he was impressed by Jean Marie's piety and love of God. Jean Marie experienced the utmost difficulty learning Latin which was required at that time to study theology. Try as he did, he was unable to master Latin grammar. Initially, he found little comfort from his classmates who would snicker and make snide remarks. One of the seminarians, Mathias Loras, endeavored to tutor Jean Marie. During one session Mathias became exasperated at Jean Marie's failure to grasp the lesson. Mathias proceeded to box his ears. Jean Marie's reaction was to humbly kneel before his tutor and beg his forgiveness. Mathias was immediately sorry for his mean temper, embracing Jean Marie. From that time on there were no gibes from his classmates. Mathias never forgot that day, even when he went on to become a bishop in America. At Father Balley's suggestion, Jean Marie undertook a sixty-two-mile pilgrimage to the shrine of St. Francis Regis for the intercession of this great saint. Jean Marie made the journey on foot, giving away all the money he had for the journey to alms seekers. Ergo, he was reduced to begging for his suppers but offering to perform some tasks in exchange. Apparently, his mission was a success. Upon his return he was met by Father Balley with a warm welcome. Thereafter, Jean Marie made encouraging progress in his studies.

CHAPTER TWO

Difficulties Along The Way

Unforseen events were to intrude uncannily on the life of Jean Marie; vicissitudes enter our lives unexpectedly. However, I maintain that nothing happens, for good or ill, fortuitously but providentially. Towards the end of 1809 Jean Marie was drafted for military service. Napoleon Bonaparte, now Emperor of France, was at war with the rest of Europe. Conscripts were desperately needed for the French army. Even though ecclesiastical students were previously exempted from service, the raging war required more cannon fodder. Father Balley appealed to the authorities to no avail. On October 26, 1809 Jean Marie reported to the military barracks in Lyons. Immediately, he was appalled by the misconduct of the soldiers and other draftees. Their course language, cursing, and scorn for religion repelled him, though he did not complain. Two days later, Jean Marie collapsed and was admitted to a hospital. His rigorous fasts and penances had taken their toll; he was bereft of strength. During the next two weeks, Father Balley, family, and friends came to visit. All Jean Marie talked about was God and his desire to become a priest. On November 12th, he was discharged from the hospital and ordered to muster with troops in the town of Roanne. He suffered a relapse and was hospitalized again. Fate was kind to him this time; it was not happenstance that the Sisters of St. Augustine ran the hospital at Roanne. Over the next six weeks Jean Marie recuperated under the tender ministrations of

11

the good sisters. Needless to say, they were favorably disposed towards him. Jean Marie would converse with the nuns about their favorite subject. His devotion to prayers and spiritual readings edified the entire community. It was with sorrow that he bid them farewell on January 5, 1810, having been ordered to report to Captain Blanchard for assignment. The next day the captain ordered Jean Marie to catch up with a regiment which had left for the Spanish frontier. He set out by himself still weak but obedient. With dusk descending, Jean Marie became confused about the directions. He was approached by a man who offered to put him up for the night. This fellow by the name of Guy later proved to be a deserter. Guy led him to the tiny village of Les Noes where he found refuge in the home of a friend of Guy. Jean Marie was given supper and a place to sleep. The next day he was introduced to the mayor who opposed the politics and martial policies of Napoleon. This man persuaded Jean Marie to remain at Les Noes. Since it was now nearly impossible to catch up with the regiment, Jean Marie reluctantly acceded. According to the law, Jean Marie was now, officially, a deserter. The mayor secured lodging for him in a hearby hamlet in the home of a widow named Claudine Fayot. In short time this mother of four children considered him a son. Jean Marie remained here for two years, hiding in the barn during the day and helping Claudine's children with their studies at night. At one time Jean Marie was almost discovered by the gendarmes who were looking for defaulters. While hiding in a haystack, Jean Marie was bayonetted but the wound was superficial.

After France defeated Austria, a temporary peace reigned in Europe. On April 2, 1810, Napoleon declared a general amnesty for all deserters. The following January, Jean Marie bid a tearful farewell to his other "mother" and his "cousins." The townsfolk insisted that he don a cassock to see what he would look like when he became a priest. In the meantime Jean Marie's brother, Francois, had enlisted in the army to take the place of Jean Marie as permitted by law. Francois, called the "Cadet" by his family, joined the military as a substitute for his brother so that the family would not be harassed by constables searching for him. Jean Marie and his family never saw him again. Jean Marie was barely home several weeks when his saintly mother died, confident that her son would one day become a priest.

Jean Marie returned to the rectory school of Father Balley where he helped with domestic chores while under the priest's tutelage. In 1812 Father Balley deemed Jean Marie suitable for studies at the minor seminary of Verrieres. There he was taught rhetoric and philosophy in his native tongue, there were about 200 students in the minor seminary who were subjected to meager meals and strict discipline. Jean Marie was lumped into a group of slow learners, where he became a fast friend of Marcellin Champognat who would one day found the Little Brothers of Mary. Marcellin also had difficulty with Latin; he, too, had made a pilgrimage to a shrine for divine guidance. Although Jean Marie was graded poor in his studies, his efforts, conduct, and character were good enough to earn him a promotion the next year to the major seminary of St. Irenee at Lyons. Here, Latin was employed in all instruction and Jean Marie faltered. He simply could not keep up with his fellow seminarians. Many days and nights he spent alone in the chapel. Within six months he was dismissed after failing the term examination.

At this juncture of his life, Jean Marie resigned

himself to the fact that it was God's will that he could not become a priest. It was the most wrenching, dolorous time of his life. Despite his mental anguish, he determined to serve God as a religious brother. With this resolve, he returned to Ecully to say goodbye to Father Balley. The wise, old priest discerned a priestly vocation in Jean Marie. For the next three months, he drilled Jean Marie for retaking the exam, reviewing the theology in French and then translating it into Latin. Upon completion of this preparation, Father Balley invited the superiors of the seminary to his rectory to test Jean Marie again. Father Balley begged them to come and they agreed. *Mirabile* dictu! (Wonderful to tell!) In his own surroundings, Jean Marie passed the examination. After an additional year of theology taught by Father Balley, Jean Marie was ready for ordination to the priesthood. Vicar-General Courbon recommended him for the priesthood with the remark that the church needed not only learned priests but holy ones. Jean Marie walked sixty miles to the Grand Seminary of Grenoble where he was ordained priest by Bishop Simon of Grenoble. The date of ordination was August 13, 1815. The following day Father Vianney offered his first mass in the seminary's chapel. Father Vianney rejoiced at how great it was to be a priest. At age twenty-nine, after many trials and hardships, Father Vianney realized his cherished dream. *Ad astra per asperum*! (To the stars through great difficulty!)

As a youth, Father Vianney had expressed a desire to become a priest so that he could win many souls to God. This fervent wish would soon be granted to him. He was assigned as assistant to Father Balley in Eculley. There was much work to be done at Eculley. Napoleon had been defeated decisively at the battle of Waterloo in Belgium in 1815.

The Eagle and Colours were superseded by the monarchial pennant of Louis XVIII. A rapproachment between state and church was compassed. Napoleon had tried to dominate Pope Pius VII by appointing bishops himself. Prelates who remained loyal to the pontiff were arrested and the seminarians in their dioceses were inducted into the army. Posthaste, seminaries were closed, the training and ordination of priests dropped precipitously. The resulting shortage of priests in France had dire consequences. With few priests to celebrate mass and administer sacraments, the religious observances of many grew slack. Fortunately, Cardinal Fisch of Lyons had secretly reopened the seminary which Father Vianney attended. So it was that God paved a path for him to fulfill his vocation.

Father Vianney greeted his first assignment with enthusiasm. He was received enthusiastically by Father Balley's flock. They were glad to have a young priest assist their aging pastor. Jean Marie offered masses, gave the children catechism lessons, visited the sick and lonely, and prepared homilies. These little catechisms on the love of God, devotion to the Blessed Mother, prayer and virtue, as well as his passionate sermons survive to this very day. During his stay at Eculley, Jean Marie learned about the discovery in the Roman catacombs of the body of the virgin martyr, St. Philomena. Jean Marie cultivated a great devotion to this saint for the rest of his life; in later years he would attribute many miracles to her powerful intercession.

Father Balley lived as an ascetic, imposing penances upon himself, including wearing the hair shirt and taking the discipline. A discipline is a scourge used for self-flagellation, the practice was completely voluntary. Father Balley exercised the discipline for mortification of the senses and reparation for sin. Father Balley would fast often; his measly meals consisted of brown bread and boiled potatoes. He seldom ate meat and never drank wine. This aged priest did not foist this severe lifestyle on his protege. Father Vianney sought to emulate his mentor in every way, sometimes to excess as he admitted late in life. Father Balley and Father Vianney shared the happiest days of their lives together. However, this joy was to be short-lived. Early in 1817, barely two years after Vianney's arrival, Father Balley developed a gangrenous ulcer on his leg. He was dead within the year. Father Vianney deeply mourned his closest friend; he attested in old age that Father Balley was the kindest, most beautiful soul he ever knew.

Although the townspeople wanted Father Vianney to be their pastor now, it was not to be so. The authorities of these matters had other plans and appointed a Father Tripier to be the pastor. In characteristic humility Vianney was thankful for the opportunity to be his assistant. This Father Tripier was the antithesis of Father Balley and Vianney. Their monastic regimen did not appeal to him. He found Vianney much too hard on himself. It is probable that he was instrumental in having Vianney transferred in a hurry. On February 9th, 1818, Father Vianney trekked to his new assignment, the poor small village of Ars. Along the road he encountered the shepherd boy, Antoin Givre, who pointed out the way. Stopping in a field Father Vianney knelt and beseeched God's blessings for his ministry. With prescience he uttered to himself that although Ars was sparsely inhabited, about 230 people comprising sixty households, someday throngs of people would visit there. Father John Vianney was now Cure of Ars.

A regeneration of the faith of the people was

needed. Since the French Revolution there was a diminution of religious observance in Ars. Subsequent to the Reign of Terror in 1794 the church of Ars was ransacked by hoodlums. It became a meeting hall for free thinkers and secularists who mockingly worshipped the goddess of Reason. There was a succession of disguised priests who performed clandestine masses and the sacraments for small groups of the faithful. After 1801 there was a gradual restoration of religious worship. Just prior to Gather Vianney's arrival, Ars was served fleetingly by a dedicated young priest, Father Deplace, who died of consumption. Most of the townsfolk were indifferent to religion. Few attended Sunday mass, preferring to stay at home or work in the fields. Few children attended catechism class. There was excessive drinking and brawling, the tiny town supporting four taverns. The people were habituated to making festivals which included public dancing; their affairs were often rowdy and randy. Generally speaking, the populace was irreligious.

Abbe Vianney was determined to improve the faith and morals of his parish. He was infused with a *fuoco divino*, a divine fire, to make possible this formidable mission. Forthwith, he visited all the families of the village, from the mayor and uppermost citizens to the lowliest peasant. Over time he endeared himself to almost everyone except the innkeepers. He helped the poor and needy, selling personal possessions. His housekeeper averred that he even gave away his mattress. She bemoaned that every time she bought fresh bread he would locate some hungry souls. Most of the time the Cure of Ars cooked for himself, subsisting on pancakes or potatoes. For the first six years at Ars, he did not take regular meals, but ate only a few times a week. Ignoring pangs of hunger, he would eat only to restore his strength never for the pleasure of eating. In old age he confessed to being imprudent in his self-denial. He endured this severe fasting to win the people back to Sunday mass and religious practice. The abbe recalled the words of Jesus concerning some evil spirits: "This kind can only be cast out by fasting." (Matthew 17:20). He abstained from meat. On one occasion his sister Marguerite visited him at his rectory with two roasted pigeons, which he refused to eat. Lest we judge him foolish or worse, let us remember the call for fasting made by our Blessed Mother during her past and present apparitions all over the world.

CHAPTER THREE

Strength From God
Through
Prayer, Good Works, Self-Discipline

Prayer was a top priority for Abbe Vianney. He would spend many hours of the day in prayer and adoration of the Blessed Sacrament in his church. Truly, he could be found almost any hour of the day or night in church, reading his Divine Office, the Lives of the Saints, and the Bible. He constantly recited the rosary, having a prodigious devotion to the Blessed Mother. As a vicaire of Ecully he had vowed to say daily the Marian prayer, *Regina Coeli* (Queen of Heaven). When looking after the sick of the parish, he would distribute rosaries and pray with the intention of their recovery. Abbe Vianney would pray on his knees in church, sometimes prostrating himself before the altar. In the pulpit he would preach loudly, but in prayer his voice was soft. He was heard to remark that when he spoke to his congregation, some were asleep or hard of hearing, but that when he prayed, he spoke to God who is not deaf. He further commented that it was easy for farmers to be saved since they could pray while they worked. Always Father Vianney would pray for the conversion of his congregation, that they would turn to God and away from sin. So great was Father Vianney's love of the Blessed Virgin since early childhood that he was blessed with apparitions of her. There are accounts in official church records of some. A certain Mademoiselle Durie assisted the cure[1] in charitable pur-

19

suits and was afflicted with cancer. One time, as she approached the cure's bedroom, she heard him talking to someone. He was pleading with the Blessed Mother to cure this woman. When Mademoiselle Durie opened the door she beheld the Blessed Mother enveloped in a dazzling light. Father Vianney was standing motionless, his countenance was radiant with his arms crossed over his breast. Mademoiselle Durie tugged at his cassock, asking who was this lady. Father Vianney confided to her that she was the Blessed Mother who promised to cure her cancer. Indeed she was cured of the cancer later on. In another church document, a fellow priest, the Abbe Toccanier, testified that Father Vianney once confided that he had a vision of the Blessed Mother near his bed. Then, again a penitent, Francois Bourdin, avowed that he had seen the Blessed Mother conversing with Father Vianney as Francois approached him for confession in the sacristy.

In addition to fasting and prayer, the holy Cure of Ars practiced self-mortification. The tradition of self-mortification is a long and venerable one originating with the desert monks of St. Anthony of Egypt and continuing through the Middle Ages. The purpose was to do penance for sin and to curb one's carnality. However, such rigorism was sometimes carried to an extreme by religious fanatics who would scourge themselves severely. This movement, known as Jensenism, was condemned as a heresy by the church. The most extreme example of such fanaticism recorded was when a young woman named Entiennette Thomasson was nailed to a cross against the wall of a church in the town of Fareins in France. Although Father Vianney scourged himself, he soundly decried the fanaticism of the Jensenists and stated that it would be easier to convert a pagan than a Jensenist. Once, a young priest, Father Tailhades, spent a few weeks with Father Vianney to learn how to be a good pastor. The Cure of Ars gave him some sound advice. He told him that the devil is not afraid of the discipline, that is, scourging oneself. What terrifies the devil is prayer and fasting. On the other hand, nothing pleases God more then prayer and fasting. Father Vianney concluded that he received extraordinary graces from God by means of prayer, good works, and fasting.

While all God-loving people realize the efficacy and spiritual rewards of prayer, few souls today are comfortable with the notion of penance and mortification. Surely, these notions are valid and confirmed in the scriptures. A definition of penance, aside from the Sacrament of Penance (now called Reconciliation), is any voluntary suffering or chastisement to show repentance for sin. The motives for penance should always be hatred of sin and expiration. Penance will cleanse the soul of past sins and guard against future ones. The necessity of penance is found in the Bible. These quotations are taken from the Holy Bible (Douay Version) printed by P.J. Kenedy and Sons, New York.: 1) Jesus Christ posits *"Do penance for the kingdom of heaven is at hand."* (Matthew 3:2) 2) Jesus declares He has come to call sinners to penance. *"I came not to call the just, but sinners to penance."* (Luke 5:32) 3) Unless we do penance we shall perish. *"But except you do penance, you shall all likewise perish."* (Luke 13:5) 4) The apostles insisted on the need for penance in preparation for baptism. *"Do penance and be baptized every one of you."* (Acts 2:38)

Mortification is the act of subduing the passions by means of renunciation, abstinence, and temperate infliction of bodily discomfort. Mortification enables us to exercise self-control, train the will, and turn our souls to God. Mortification is Scripture based: 1) *"Every one of you that does not renounce all that he possesses cannot be my disciple." (Luke 14:33)* 2) *Leaving all things they followed him." (Luke 5:11)* *"If any man will come after me, let him deny himself."* (Luke 9:23) 3) *"Mortify therefore your members."* (Colossians 3:5) 4) *"But if by the spirit you mortify the deeds of the flesh, you shall live."* (Romans 8:13) 5) *"They that are Christ's have crucified their flesh, with the vices and concupiscences."* (Galatians 5:24)

I proffer a personal opinion on the subject. In our hedonistic, materialistic culture, we have an aversion to any thought of penance and mortification. Necessarily, it is time to reconsider. Immoderate indulgence in penance and mortification betokens spiritual gluttony and lust. The perpetrator is seeking consolation from God and/or others. The font of such illicit desire is found in pride.

Notwithstanding the emerging popularity of Father John Vianney among the people of Ars, he had his detractors. Father Vianney railed against the bar owners from his first days in Ars; they, in turn, did not suffer him gladly. If the bars were just places of harmless amusement, Father Vianney would not have castigated them. However, the men of the town would assemble in them (even on Sunday without going to mass) and get roaringly drunk. Then they would swear, curse, and fight. Eventually they would return home, often becoming abusive to their wives and children. (Battered women and children is not a recent phenomenon.) Father Vianney remonstrated that Sunday was a time for church worship and fellowship. He accused the innkeepers of stealing the bread of a poor woman and her children by selling wine to drunkards who spend on Sunday what they earn during the week. Another abuse condemned by the cure[1] were the public dances in the village square held on holidays and sometimes Sundays. These affairs became occasions of ribaldry, vanity, and intoxication. Blasphemies, that is, cursing and swearing, were commonplace. Father Vianney chided adults who attended these dances for endangering their own morals as well as their children. He warned that these events promoted immodest dress for maidens and impure behavior for both sexes, thus compromising their virtue. Worse still, the sensual appetites and passions becoming inflamed by bawdy entertainment, were nearly impossible to control, therefore: *Otempora*! *Omores*! (What times! What customs!) How would the good cure[1] react to today's salacious spectacles in topless bars and disco dance floors, pornography and lewd behavior? How well Father Vianney understood human nature and what happens when freedom disintegrates into license.

The innkeepers, together with some disgruntled patrons, soon mounted a counterattack. In 1823 Bishop Devie, the ordinary of the diocese of Belley which included Ars, received anonymous letters of complaint about Father Vianney. These letters defamed his reputation, alleging he was guilty of concealed prurience. His defamers even went so far as to enlist the help of a disreputable woman who vilified Father Vianney publicly. The bishop had no choice but to investigate the charges. Of course, none of these allegations were true and the cure was exonerated after an official church inquiry. The slanderers were silenced, but Father Vianney was heart-broken. The scandal caused him to wish to leave Ars, but his many supporters prevailed upon him to stay. The ordeal had a positive effect. It prompted Father

Vianney to forgive the wrongdoers and pray for them. He exclaimed that we should pray for a love of the cross, then it will become sweet. The good people of Ars, and they were the majority, rallied behind their pastor; this misfortune spurred growing admiration for him. Thus, once again, merciful God had drawn good from evil.

CHAPTER FOUR

Spiritual Warfare
and
Temporal Welfare

And now we come to a most horrifying part of Father Vianney's life. Although he was never again maligned by townsfolk, he was oppressed by our arch enemy. From 1824 to 1858, a span of 35 years, the Cure of Ars suffered vicious, overt attacks by devils. The existence of Satan, of fallen angels, of a hell of everlasting torment are doctrines of the Catholic Church. The evidence of the existence of evil forces, powers of darkness, especially in the twentieth century, seems overwhelming. In fewer than a hundred years, mankind has endured two world wars, in addition to numerous other wars. The world has seen the systematic killing of millions of innocent men, woman, and children. Organized genocide and ethnic cleansing of whole peoples in Europe, Africa, and Asia has flourished. Ponder the unthinkable crimes against humanity committed during the Holocaust, and on a lesser scale in Cambodia, Rwanda, and Bosnia. Untold destruction, suffering, and death have taken place and continue to take place. And, now, mankind is confronted with a grave new peril, one which will claim millions of lives everywhere in the world - the virulent plague of AIDS. This horrendous evil does not issue from God but from the Evil One. Satan and his legions have engineered this unparalleled misery through the diabolical actions of human beings. A multitude of corrupted souls have become his instruments of evil.

Now the question is why did the devil wage unremitting warfare against the cure[1] for thirty-five long years. I submit it was precisely because Abbe Vianney had become a principal foe. A possessed woman once shrieked to him that if there were three people on earth like himself, Satan's kingdom would be destroyed. Satan was furious that Abbe Vianney was leading so many souls to salvation. The Cure[1] of Ars could not be corrupted, could not be persuaded to do evil, although he was subject to temptation and vexation. Because Abbe Vianney was so good and influenced others to be good, he was targeted for the undying hatred of the Evil One. The following events have been documented during the process of his beatification and canonization as a saint.

In the beginning, Father Vianney was not aware that he was beset by devils. When there were mysterious sounds in the rectory, he suspected rodents. When he heard shouts in his bedroom, he inferred that thieves were breaking in. But no, these disturbances did not emanate from earthly culprits. Becoming somewhat unnerved, Father Vianney asked the town's wheelwright, Andre Verchere, to spend an evening with him. After they had retired, heavy blows were struck against the house walls and the whole house shook violently. Andre declined to stay another night. Father Vianney came to the conclusion this was the work of Satan since God would not want to frighten him. Soon after, the demons became more bold; they shoved the furniture around, growling like wild beasts. Although they remained invisible, these infernal spirits spoke to Father Vianney in ugly voices. Shouting epithets and insults, they would pull him out of his bed and drag him around the room. Other people besides Andre Verchere bore witness to these terrifying occurrences. His sister Marguerite visited him, spending the night in the presbytery. She recounted that she was awakened by a tremendous noise near her bed, on the table and cupboard. Neighbors heard these terrific noises in their own homes and rendered testimony of such. One time some fellow priests, who were incredulous, left their own parishes to stay with Father Vianney. In the middle of the night, amidst rumbling noises, the whole rectory shook as if there were an earthquake. When they rushed into Father Vianney's bedroom, they discovered his heavy bed had been dragged into the middle of the room. These infestations persisted throughout Father Vianney's life, culminating in a bizarre conflagration two years before he died. On February 24, 1857, while Father Vianney was hearing confessions in the church, a fire broke out in the rectory in his bedroom. His bed and bed curtains were consumed in the flames. What is truly amazing is that the fire started and halted by itself. Villagers who were passing by the presbytery saw the blaze through a window. No one put out the fire, yet it died out without engulfing the entire bedroom. Holy objects on a chest of drawers were spared.

The Cure[1] of Ars was stoic in the face of this malevolent aggression. He ascribed Satan's vengeance to the fact that so many souls were being saved. Often the infernal spirits groaned he was robbing them of their share of souls. They would curse and call him names, like black toad. In response to this invective, Father Vianney would make the Sign of the Cross, rebuke Satan in the name of Jesus, and pray his rosary.

It must be stressed that the Blessed Mother was a powerful advocate of Father Vianney. That she safeguarded him was reassured publicly on January 23,

1840. The cure[1] was hearing the confession of a woman; there were about ten people waiting to go to confession who heard what transpired. An account is related by Catherine Lassagne, one of the penitents. At first the woman remained silent, then screamed at Father Vianney that she was *Magister caput*! (The Master!) In a chilling voice tones the possessed woman denounced the cure[1] for aggrieving "The Chief!" and insisted that he leave the parish. Then the demon inside her cried out that Father Vianney was protected from harm by that (here it used a filthy expletive) Lady up above.

After a third of a century Satan finally gave up tormenting him, utterly defeated. Father Vianney vanquished Satan through his ardent love of God and fellow man. During this stretch of years the Cure[1] of Ars toiled unceasingly for the spiritual and temporal welfare of his parishioners. In 1820 he set about restoring the old church of Ars. A new altar and side chapels were installed; pictures and statues of saints were added; over the chapel dedicated to Saint John the Baptist he had inscribed, "His head was the price of a dance." The cure[1] had a vision of the future in renovating the church when thousands of pilgrims would visit. He wanted a glorious house for God, nothing for his rectory or himself. He wanted people to feel exalted while in church and believed that sometimes the mere sight of the tabernacle, holy pictures, and other furnishings could convert a sinner. The cure[1] paid for these improvements himself with a small inheritance he received when his father died. Moreover, he would appeal to the congregation, especially wealthy benefactors. He had a canvas hung near the sacristy with this epigraph: *"Give and it shall be given unto you."* (Luke 6:38).

Father Vianney did not ignore the education of

the youth of Ars and its environs. In November 1824, he purchased a small house near the church which was used as a school. The students were orphans and destitute waifs who were given free room and board. The house was named *La Providence*. It was school and domicile for up to sixty girls who were taught skills to make a living. Father Vianney selected two young teachers, Catherine Lassagne and Benorte Lardet, who worked for no salary. They had studied with the sisters of St. Joseph at Fareins. Though these single women professed no vows they lived a chaste, holy life at *La Providence*. In fact, Catherine Lassagne had come under the spell of the good cure[1] when she was twelve years old when he would give children catechism lessons in the kitchen of the rectory. Catherine was the headmistress of the school for a duration of twenty-two years. She esteemed Father Vianney, who would sometimes prove intractable. One time he brought a homeless child to her when there were no vacant beds. Catherine called his attention to this fact. He gently retorted that she should be willing to sacrifice her own. *La Providence* soon gained a wonderful reputation. Its graduates went on to find good jobs, married, and became mothers; some even entered religious life. It is documented that a lawyer from Lyons who visited *La Providence* in 1841 wrote a glowing report. His digest stated that the institution sheltered some fifty to sixty girls between the ages of twelve and eighteen. The girls came from all parts, were admitted without payment, stayed for an unlimited period, and were finally placed in the farms of surrounding districts. Moreover, these girls formed a larger family in which the older members taught the younger both by example and by counsel. This was no ordinary institution. It was truly the product of the holiness of its founder.

Father Vianney did not overlook the education of the boys in his parish. He persuaded the mayor to hire an exemplary teacher for the village school, a position he held for fourteen years. Father Vianney would often pay the tuition of needy boys. On March 10, 1849 the abbe's dream for a Catholic school became a reality. The superior remained for forty-one years and became a close friend of the cure. Though Father Vianney had received little schooling when he was a child, he was a proponent of education and labored yeomanly for the cause. In so doing, he prepared a host of disadvantaged youngsters for law-abiding, productive lives.

The transformation of Ars through Abbe Vianney's succor has been documented by pilgrims who flocked to see this holy priest of God. They were awed by the tranquility and peace of the place. Here, more than elsewhere, one seemed to breathe a genial atmosphere; the inhabitants always gave them a kindly greeting. When they asked to be directed, advice was eagerly tendered. Everyone was indeed imbued with goodwill towards everybody else. Pilgrims testified they would walk through the fields at harvest time and never hear a coarse word. Swearing, drunkenness, and fisticuffs were ancient history. The men and women had become reserved and gracious. When a pilgrim expressed praise, a peasant replied that the people of Ars were no better than other towns, but surely it would be too shameful a thing to commit sin when they lived so close to a saint. The townspeople cooperated with each other in every instance and joined together at religious devotions. Abbe Vianney loved those feast days very much because people came to church without compulsion, urged solely by the fervor of a more perfect love. A major feast day was *Corpus Christi* (Body of Christ). Townspeople and pilgrims would march together with Abbe Vianney at the head of the procession. Try to visualize this heavenly pageant. He is appareled resplendently in Corpus Christi vestments, carrying a silver monstrance containing the Holy Eucharist. The crowd would be singing Hosanna in the Highest. At the tinkling of a bell, all would become silent and kneel. They bow their heads as Abbe Vianney lifts the monstrance aloft and blesses them with it. The crowd rises to its feet and resumes singing with refrains of Alleluias reaching a crescendo. Clouds of smoke curl skyward from censer, with the Cure of Ars under a golden canopy while the procession winds its way to church.

With the passage of forty years this tireless priest heard the confessions of countless people. By the end of his life, 100,000 pilgrims a year were coming to Ars. Today, 500,000 people of all religious denominations make the pilgrimage. Men and women young and old streamed into his confessional box where he spent fifteen hours a day, sometimes more. They poured out their hearts, disclosing their sins, problems, and suffering. It is accorded he consoled them with true priestly tenderness; it was a joy to him to wipe away their tears. All came away from him with a mind more serene and a spirit strengthened to fight the battle of life. It is also agreed that Abbe Vianney possessed supernormal intuition and could read the hearts and minds of penitents, even when he confessed perfect strangers. Furthermore, he could predict future events in their lives with astounding accuracy. People consulted him about their vocations, family complications, illnesses, and decisions that had to be made. He knew the conscience and interior dispositions of these people. So strong was the general feeling imputing to him supernatural powers that no one ever hesitated to give credence to his words. The following harrowing happening is recorded in church archives.

There was a young woman who sought Father Vianney's counsel about procuring employment. Before she said a word he told her that she was headed for the city of Lyons to find work. He apprised there was great danger for her there. He pleaded for her to think of him and pray to God when in peril. When the young woman reached Lyons, she went to the registry office to seek employment. A man there informed her that he was looking for a maid. At the appointed hour she went to his home at La Merlatiere. On the threshold she beheld the man who had engaged her, motioning her to enter. Suddenly, she was seized with an immense terror. Remembering the priest's words, she called out to God and fled. The man pursued her but was unable to catch her. Shortly after she learned that she barely escaped the hands of the notorious Dumollard, who had earned for himself the nickname of the murderer of servant girls. When the criminal was apprehended, she gave evidence against him in court. Of course, she returned to Father Vianney to thank him for saving her life.

Another attestation of the cure's ability to predict the future concerns two young women who journeyed to assist in his catechism class. At the conclusion of the lesson, Father Vianney called one of the girls aside. He cautioned her to keep watch over her companion on their return to their native village. He foresaw a calamity befalling her. He admonished them both to receive Holy Communion which they did. On their way home the doomed girl was bitten by a poisonous snake along the road. She expired almost immediately. Although Father Vianney did not know what would be the cause or the details surrounding her demise, his intuition of impending disaster was correct. He consoled the poor child's family with the assurance that the girl went to heaven as she had just taken Holy Communion. There were other times when God allowed Father Vianney to see clearly the particulars of an imminent peril, so that he could prescribe steps to avoid it.

CHAPTER FIVE

Fruits of Holiness

The Catholic Church maintains that its members belong to an extended family on earth called the Church. But there is also a heavenly family called the communion of saints which we hope to embosom when we depart this life. Actually, this communion extends to all who share in the life of Christ whether here or in the hereafter. Catholics believe that our love and help for each other reach beyond the grave. This is why we entreat the deceased saints to pray for us just as we ask the prayers and good intentions of the living. It must be noted that when we seek prayers from others, these prayers are directed through Christ to God. Ultimately, it is God who answers our prayers. Saints come from every race, religion,and background. They may have been clergy or laity, celibate or married. The only prerequisite is the stamp of holiness. We are all called to become saints, though it is very rare to be declared one by the church.

The Catholic Church is circumspect in its proclamation of sainthood for an individual. A person must undergo a long, exacting process of beatification and canonization before being recognized formally as a saint. In addition to heroic sanctity, there is a requirement of at least two miracles through their intercession. A miracle is an event or effect that contradicts scientific laws and is thought to be due to an act of God. Miracles engendered by saints usually involve physical cures which defy medical explanation.

Rectory (Vianney's Domicile)

Kitchen of Rectory

Interior of old church (notice crutches of persons who where healed)

Vianney's Bed (Where he died)

The shrine of Saint John Vianney

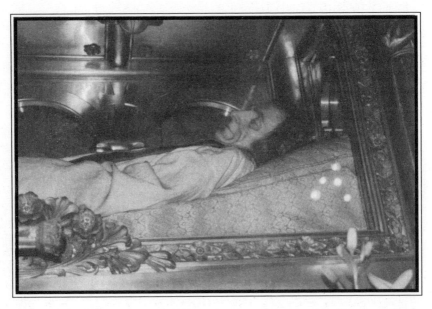

The Saint's incorupt body (a mask is covering his actual face)

At least thirty miracles were credited to Abbe Vianney, including seventeen cures after his death. Thousands of pilgrims flooded Ars each year with broken bodies, mental illness, and all sorts of maladies seeking his intercession. Healing sick babies was not his first priority, curing souls through a spiritual healing was most important to him. Abbe Vianney posited that God is always almighty; He can at all times work miracles, and He would work them now as in days of old were it not that faith is wanting. Evaluated for authenticity during his process of beatification were miracles including the cure of a nun's tuberculous, a child's growth in the throat, a woman's paralyzed left arm, a man's paralyzed legs, a child who had been blind two years, and another child who was completely deaf and blind. One miracle that caused quite a stir throughout the country happened to Abbe Vianney himself.

When the holy servant of God celebrated the Mass, he sometimes experienced rapture, a state of mystical union with God. At these times he would be surrounded by an unearthly brightness, his face transfixed and encircled by an aureole. On one occasion Abbe Vianney experienced the phenomenon called levitation, that is, he rose and remained in the air without any natural support. This most remarkable grace was witnessed by Canon Gardette, chaplain to the Carmelites of Charlon-sur-Saone. He testified that his brother and he made a pilgrimage to Ars. In the evening while Abbe Vianney recited night prayers, they took up a position facing the pulpit. About the middle of the exercise, when the cure[1] was saying his act of charity, his brother, whose eyesight is excellent, saw him rise in the air, little by little, until his feet were above the ledge of the pulpit. The abbe's countenance was transfigured and encircled by an aureole.

As soon as they came out of the church the Chaplain's brother could no longer refrain from speaking of the prodigy which he had beheld with his own eyes: he spoke of it to all who wished to hear, and with much alacrity.

One of the most celebrated miracles took place in 1829. The heat that summer was intense, and the sunbaked farms produced a paltry harvest. The supply of corn at *La Providence* had dwindled to a few handfuls stored in the attic. Despite the begging cup of Father Vianney, there was no money to purchase more. Father Vianney's faith in God's beneficence remained steadfast. He rounded up the orphans to pray together for their daily bread. After a while, he asked the cook, Jeanne-Marie Chanay, to gather the corn in the attic. She returned stunned with disbelief. There was a huge pyramid of corn in the attic, so much so that she could scarcely open the door. The attic was overflowing with corn.

All of these miracles became the talk of France, fueling speculation that a living saint dwelled in Ars. In 1840 in Lyons a special booking office was opened for trains running to Ars to accommodate the throngs of pilgrims. By 1855, two packed trains ran daily. The pilgrims who could not find room in a hotel would sleep in the meadows or on the steps of the church, waiting to go to confession and mass.

During the last year of Abbe Vianney's life, over a hundred thousand pilgrims journeyed to Ars to receive blessings and confession. The journalist, Mr. Georges Seigneur, reported his experience in the confessional. As he knelt he heard an indescribable sob issue from the abbe. Was it an exclamation of pain? Or a cry of love? Every so often the sob was repeated. Sheer exhaustion wrung that plaintiff cry from the abbe. Yet his cry of pain became one of love, and the sensible effort of a soul crushed by earth to open for itself a way to heaven. Abbe Vianney never once neglected or stinted in his priestly duties.

The Cure[1] of Ars had a singular love for the poor. He managed to pay the rent of at least thirty indigent families. He sold everything he owned to feed the hungry. He would take those in rags into his room and give them clothes. One day he met someone on the road who was barefoot; off came his shoes.

The cure[1] was happy when paupers came to his door so that he didn't have to spend time looking for them. Acutely aware of their sensibilities, the cure[1] was always discreet in his charity, considering the poor his friends. In his old age the Cure[1] of Ars was invested by Bishop Chalandon on October 25, 1852, with the mozetta, a silken shoulder cape, in recognition of his work. The cure[1] was thus elevated to the position of honorary canon over his protestations of being undeserving. Soon after the bishop's departure the cure[1] sold the apparel for fifty francs which he dispensed to the poor. Throughout his life Father Vianney had a great love for the poor which stemmed from his great love of God. In a homeless beggar he saw Jesus Christ in a distressing disguise.

By the summer of 1859 Abbe Vianney knew he was dying; in fact he predicted the exact date of his death, August 4th, 1859. He was perfectly conscious and remained so to the end. He made his confession with his wonted devotion. Nor was the devil permitted to torment him in this victorious hour. Having taken the Host in Holy Viaticum, he whispered that it was sad to receive Holy Communion for the last time. At two o'clock in the morning while a storm with lightning and thunder broke over the village of Ars, this extraordinary servant of God surrendered his soul to his beloved God, living out one of his most profound sayings, "How sweet it is to die if one has lived on the cross."

Forty-five years later, in 1904, the body of the cure[1] was exhumed as part of an official examination of his life and holiness. The body was found to be incorrupt. His course was advanced by the testimony of many witnesses as to his virtue and confirmation of the many miracles that redound to his credit. On the joyous Feast of Pentecost, May 31, 1925, the humble, tireless servant of God was canonized a saint by Pope Pius XI. These words were addressed to a concourse of thousands assembled in St. Peter's Square as the bells of all the churches pealed: "We declare to be a saint and we enroll in the catalogue of the saints the Blessed Jean-Marie Baptiste Vianney.

Since the death of Saint Vianney, seventeen more miraculous cures have been attributed to his intercession. Undoubtedly, he continues to do good from heaven. To his eternal tribute, Saint Vianney is considered patron saint of all parish priests of the world, so that his glory will be reflected upon all those whose life is dedicated to the salvation of souls.

Although Saint Vianney died well over a hundred years ago, if he were alive today his life would still proclaim the same message to the entire world. He would appeal to humanity to come back to goodness and to God. Come back from being obsessed with money, power, and pleasure to being spiritual with sound values. Come back from materialism to compassion and charity. Come back from self-indulgence to self-sacrifice. In fine, to come back from worldly false values and standards of success, to a genuine love of God demonstrated by love and service to other people.

In concluding the personal history and spiritual journey of Saint John Vianney, I would like to present some of his profound thoughts on nurturing our spiritual life. Paramount in his teachings was the need for love of God and neighbor. Saint Vianney extolled God's love for us and our reciprocal love for God. God needs nothing from us; all He desires is our love, a love reflected in service to others. We were created in an act of love, it suffuses our essence. To be unloving is to be contrary to our very being. When we are hostile or hateful, we are miserable. Sin effaces our lovingness. When we are sinful, we stifle love and are in thrall of Satan, causing abject misery. Pity the soul which has lost love, the ability to give or receive it.

Saint Vianney emphasized God's mercy. Our sins are like a grain of sand beside God's mountain of mercy. When we sin we should forthwith reconcile ourselves with God, who forgives a repentant sinner unconditionally. Saint Vianney was prone to using metaphors and parables in his preaching. He asserted that God would pardon a repentant sinner more quickly than a mother would snatch a child out of a fire. He compared God's mercy to an overflowing torrent carrying away hearts with it. When we commit sin we weave thorns around our hearts.

Citing the need for the sacrament of Reconciliation, Saint Vianney tells this story. There was a hungry wolf that came into the county devouring everything. He seized a child in its mouth and carried it off. Some men who were working nearby attacked the wolf and snatched the child. It is thus that the sacrament of Reconciliation rescues us from the claws of the devil. Saint Vianney alluded to the devil and our guardian angel as secretaries. The devil writes down our bad actions to accuse us of them; our guardian angel writes down our good deeds to justify us on the Day of Judgment.

Saint Vianney acclaims the Holy Spirit our light and strength. The Holy Spirit teaches us to distinguish between truth and falsehood and between good and evil. The blessed Mother is like a beautiful gleam of sun on a foggy day. She places herself between God and us, staying God's just punishment of sinners with her pleas for pardon. The Blessed Virgin is like a mother who has many children (She is everyone's mother!) and is perpetually tending to the needs of each child. Saint Vianney salutes the priest as the selfless steward of God. The priest is not a priest for himself. He does not administer the sacraments to himself. He does not preach, teach, perform the spiritual and corporal works of mercy to himself. The role of the priest, like Christ, is to sacrifice himself in love to others. If the priest could understand the greatness of his office, he would die not of fear, but of love. When we see a priest, we should think of Jesus Christ.

Saint Vianney trumpets the help of saints and angels. It is God's will that saints should be our protectors and our friends. They are always ready to come to our aid when we call upon them. Those whom we invoke watch over us at all times. The friendship of saints fills us with love for God. The saints love everyone. Their hearts, inflamed with divine love, are dilated in proportion to the number of souls God puts in their way. Our guardian angels are our most faithful friends, because they are with us day and night, always and everywhere. We ought often to invoke them. With what humility should we assist at mass, if we realized that our guardian angel was kneeling beside us, prostrate before the majesty of God! With what eagerness should we not ask him to offer our prayers to Jesus Christ! All the saints and angels are engaged in trying to prevent us from committing sin. Do not try to please everybody. Try to please God, the saints and the angels, they are your public.

Saint Vianney would rhapsodize over the inestimable merit and benefits of frequent reception of holy communion. The Eucharist is the bread of life which nourishes us spiritually. To attend mass without communicating worthily is the same as attending a banquet without eating. Jesus Christ offers His very own Body and Blood to inhere in us. When we receive holy communion worthily, we are inundated with God's love. To receive holy communion worthily is the most loving act possible, greater than a work of mercy. Adoration of God before the blessed sacrament in church is another supreme act of love for God. Saint Vianney would spend time each day, often prostrate on the floor, before the tabernacle. He professed his love for God with oral and silent prayer. In mediation we open our hearts to God so that God can speak to us in the stillness of our souls. How dismaying to think that adoration of the blessed sacrament has been almost abandoned by many Catholics. More disturbing is that a sizable percentage of Catholics do not believe in the real presence of Christ in the Holy Eucharist. Let us pray for an increase of faith for these Christians so that they may believe and sense the realness of Christ when receiving Holy Communion.

Recently, I was thunderstruck by a book entitled, *Eucharistic Miracles*, written by Joan Carroll Cruz and published by Tan Books of Rockford, Illinois. This illustrated book delineates thirty-six major Eucharistic miracles in Church history. The author talks of hosts which have turned to visible flesh, hosts which have bled, hosts which have levitated, and many other miracles. The author details the official investigations into these phenomena as well as where the hosts can be seen and venerated today.

To receive holy communion frequently, a person must need go to confession regularly, at least once a month. We are all sinners, and we sin all the time. Hopefully, most of our sins are venial but we also commit mortal sins at times. When we fall into grievous sin, we should rush to confession without hesitation. Even lesser sins should be confessed as soon as possible. Sin blackens the soul, making it ugly and displeasing to God. Though our sins be as scarlet, confession and resolution will make them white as snow. We must try to make a good confession, never deliberately hiding or omitting any sin. It goes without saying, we must be remorseful and determined not to sin again.

It is a paradox to me to see so many people at mass communicating, while so few go to confession, especially young people. Can it be that most Catholics no longer lapse into sin, or is it that we have lost our sense of sin and guilt for their commission. I trust no warning is necessary: to knowingly receive Holy Communion in a state of serious sin is, ipso facto, a very grave sin. Profanation of the sacrament is a sacrilege.

Saint Vianney was ever mindful of the horrible consequences of sin. Moral perversity will wreak suffering and death. Saint Paul was keenly aware of this truth in his conviction, *"The wages of sin is death."* (Romans 6:23) Saint Vianney reproved sinners not to be harsh or judgmental, but to correct and remedy. He would spend fifteen hours of each day hearing confession and helping people work out their salvation. He would counsel penitents to pray, fast, and avoid temptation.

In this life we are engaged in spiritual warfare; our

adversaries are Satan, an evil system of things, and our own evil inclinations. We must purge ourselves of sinful habits and steel our will not to sin. With the grace of God, we can defeat the devil, resist the temptations of the world,and overcome our sinful inclinations. Every day we should examine our conscience. Have we sinned through pride, avarice, lust, envy, gluttony, or anger? Every day we should reflect on our mortality, and the account we must render to our merciful, yet just, God. St. Paul sounded the alarm and wake up call: *"It is appointed unto men once to die, and after this the judgment."* (Hebrews 9:27)

I would like to interject the four last things that should be on our minds: death, judgment, heaven, or hell. Every day we should labor for our salvation, with the confidence that God desires as much. *"For God hath not appointed us unto wrath, but unto the purchasing of salvation by our Lord Jesus Christ."* (I Thessalonians 5:9) Every day we should think of our *summum bonum* - to be in paradise with God and the company of saints. Like the saints, don't we have the same God to help us, the same heaven to hope for, the same hell to fear?

PART TWO

Today's Church and World

"So we being many, are one body in Christ, and every one members of one another." Romans 12:15

CHAPTER SIX

The Ten Commandments:
A Blueprint For Life

What is the relevance of Saint Vianney's life and thoughts for today's church and world? The answer is simple. His traditional sanctity and teachings can be applied to modern issues and ministry. Saint Vianney was the personification of Catholic theology. He adhered to the Bible, the church fathers, and the giants of classical Western spirituality, Saint Augustine and Saint Thomas Aquinas. Saint Vianney espoused orthodox church teachings concerning the sacraments and grace. His sermons and catechism, rich with parables and metaphors, addressed the real-life situation and problems of his parishioners. But one might object that the church and world is radically different from that which existed 200 years ago. And what of the metamorphosis in Catholicism since the Second Vatican Council?

Saint Vianney's impassioned response would be that the Bible, Catholic dogma, and the church magisterium (teaching authority) are not outdated or irrelevant today. The Catholic Church serves all Catholics everywhere for all time. This was guaranteed by its founder, Jesus Christ, speaking to its first pope, Saint Peter. *"And I say to thee: Thou art Peter; and upon this rock I will build my church, and the gates of hell shall not prevail against it."* (Matthew 16:18) There is no such thing as a new morality for today but only a lack of it. People are accountable for their actions as much now as they were in the days of Moses. We continue to be richly rewarded and justly punished by God. The church teaches us what we must do in our relationship with God and fellow man: love God with thy whole heart, soul, and strength; love thy neighbor as thyself. One might object that this is an oversimplification of church teachings. Saint Vianney would respond that this love of God, as reflected in good works, is the wellspring of church teachings and sacraments, the rest is commentary.

Only from the summit of spiritual ecstasy can we fathom the meaning of privation of God. It is the utter lack of suitability for being a human being. Whensoever a person loses sight of God and becomes an anguished creature of despair, full of self-pity and contempt, then that person has severed, temporarily or permanently, his relationship with God. If the despair persists the person becomes hardened in his sins, bereft of free-will, and an instrument of the Evil One.

In our present day, the principal socializing institutions of man, the family, organized religion, the schools, and laws and customs of society are in a state of upheaval and disarray. Modern civilization is eroding because of incessant warfare, barbarism, and depravity. The spectre of nuclear obliteration still hangs over all of us. Man craves to find truth and peace, but treachery and truculence abound. Many people have subverted their essential goodness to pander to their base instincts and prejudices.

Pope John XXIII, a man of vision who perceived the inertia existing in the Catholic Church, the accumulation of ages of formalism, was determined to open the windows and clear out the cobwebs. In initiating the Second Vatican Council he valiantly set forth the forces of revitalization through *aggiornamento*, which translates into a rebirth of, or renewal, of the Christian ethos. Reexamination and restructuring of church dogma were undertaken with pentecostal and ecumenical fervor to mirror the infinite love and mercy of God.

The teachings of Jesus Christ, exemplified in the life of Saint Vianney, are salutary for all people *howsoever His person is perceived by anyone.* Whether He is recognized as the divine Son of God by Christians, a great prophet by Moslems, a master rabbi by a multitude of Jews, Jesus Christ was a wonderful teacher. Like Saint Vianney, He taught moral precepts by means of parables. These memorable stories highlighted moral truths and defined clearly right and wrong behavior. In drawing another parallel with Saint Vianney, our blessed Savior would expound His teaching using concrete, realistic situations everyone comes to experience. In no uncertain terms, Christ would contrast virtuous and sinful actions and reactions of people in these situations. There was never ambiguity or equivocation in the sermons of Jesus Christ or Saint Vianney. Their code of ethics was not situational but absolute; their love of others and service to them were absolute.

Because we are weak in the spirit and flesh, we often capitulate to the nefarious designs of Lucifer, whose power is immense in this epoch of the great apostasy and tribulation. These are the times of fulfillment, the eschaton, predicted in the Bible. Because we transgress against God, fellow man and selves, we must bear the retribution of a just God and an impassible cosmos.

Because we have doubt to the point of despair, we endure, at times, the agony of separation, of turning our backs, to our Creator. But because God loves us and desires our love for Him, He sees fit day-in and day-out to restore hope in us. In confidence and trust in our Father's longing for us, we must wend our way through temporal life to eternal life. Faith, alone, is not enough. We must embrace God's revealed truths and do all that is virtuous and charitable in spite of our natural inclination to selfishness and wrongdoing. In so doing, God will give us the strength needed to rebuke the forces of Evil: upon death we will rest forever in the bosom of our loving Father.

Judaic-Christian moral precepts are promulgated in the Hebrew and Christian scriptures as well as the Mishna and oral tradition which flowered after the scriptures were composed. With all the respective cachets of Judaism and Christianity, the inextricably entwined roots of these religions derive from the ten commandments. Ultimately, the tenets and structures of these faiths flow from the Decalogue which is their foundation. Every Jew and Christian is bound by covenant and conscience to observe the ten commandments found in the Books of Exodus (20:2-17) and Deuteronomy (5:6-21).

Indubitably, these moral precepts are the bedrock of all religions. The holy writ of all religions prescribe virtuous conduct and enjoin wicked behavior. Moral laws are embedded in the infrastructure of all societies, in their cultural mores and jurisprudence. The purport of religion is to communicate a here-and, now presence of God in the world and to help us draw closer to Him. God shows Himself in all of life, creation and history. God continues to radiate, although our vision is clouded by the way we live in today's world. The lofty ideal of world peace and brotherhood is hampered by global armament, fierce competitiveness, and an inequitable distribution of wealth, which precipitates warfare, national hatreds, and subjugation of weaker people. The *raison d'etre* of religion is to impel us to conform to God's will. Circumstances will change, our life styles will change, the whole social order has changed, but God's love for us is constant and everlasting. We can respond to His love in our daily lives through the faithful practice of our religion.

Some people scoff that the ten commandments as a basis for morality is outdated in today's world. They maintain that adhering to a moral code set forth thousands of years ago is untenable, that ethics are situational and not absolute. They fail to perceive that their own stance is absolute in itself.

Jesus said, *"If you wish to enter into life, keep the commandments."* (Matthew 19:17) The apostle John wrote, *"The man who claims, `I have known Him' (God) without keeping his commandments, is a liar; in such a one there is no truth."* (I John 2:4) He goes on to write: *"One who has no love for the brother he has seen cannot love the God he has not seen. The commandment we have from him is this: whoever loves God must also love his brother."* (I John 4:20-21) The ten commandments are spiritual conduits for a successful, abundant life. The two great commandments are a dichotomy of the same substance: Love toward God and love toward neighbor. The entire Bible exudes the love of God for man, it is His love letter to all mankind. Jesus Christ is the personification of God's love. He said *"You will live in my love if you keep my commandments, even as I have kept my Father's commandments and live in His love."* (John 15:10) God's ten commandments constitute a universal law of love. *"Love is the fulfillment of the Law."* (Romans 13:10) Through observing the ten commandments, we can manifest the mighty spiritual law of love that Jesus bade: love God and your fellow man with all your heart. Love is the very quintessence of the ten commandments and the foundation of all religions. We can be sure of our union and fellowship with God by keeping His commandments: *"But whoever keeps his (God's) word, truly has the love of God been made perfect in Him."* (I John 2:5)

CHAPTER SEVEN

Commandments Encompassing
our
Relationship with God

I am now going to propound, for your consideration, the relevance of the ten commandments to our lives in today's world as members of the Catholic Church. The order and wording varies with the Bible of our Protestant brethren, but the core message is the same. In elucidating the pertinence of these commandments I should like to compose brief apologies in like fashion with the moral stories and parables of Saint John Vianney. In addition, I will include his thoughts on the sins we commit when we break these commandments.

The First Commandment: *"I am the Lord thy God, Who brought thee out of the land of Egypt, out of the house of bondage. Thou shalt not have strange gods before Me."*

There are false gods worshipped by people throughout the world. Superstition is rampant with multitudes of people ascribing magical powers to animate and inanimate things. Animism is the belief that spirits dwell in things and must be propitiated, or, else, they will become malevolent towards humans.

Technology has become a god to many people. Machines, division of labor, and automation have enabled the production of enormous quantities of material goods for dissemination to people around the globe. Making goods via machines has resulted in the gradual disappearance of crafts and jobs requiring manual skills. Computerization has obviated the demand for people, except as overseers of the computers, in innumerable systems of production. As the human element decreases, the dependence on machines increases. Productivity and accountability are measured exactly in a quantitative and objective way when dealing with machines. Input and output can be gauged and controlled with precision, and hardly ever with error. This is not possible with humans who are not as hard working, efficient, reliable, or manageable. A direct result is that people are being replaced by machines. Persons losing their jobs, whose skills are no longer marketable, are hard pressed to be "retooled" for other work. Another pejorative consequence is that technology has become a magical god worshipped by people who opine that everything can be made all right if the proper buttons are pushed.

More false gods are the philosophies of naturalism and humanism. Naturalists posit nature, the material order, as the ultimate reality. Nature is in a slow but steady state of flux called evolution, of which man is a part. The humanists elaborate on this theory by making man the preeminent figure in the grand scheme of things. People who subscribe to this philosophy aver that man is entirely self-sufficient, and per se, not dependent upon a supreme being. They do not believe in the existence of God and, therefore, deny any relationship between man and his Creator.

Since the naturalist limits his perspective to what can be gleaned from sensory data and cognition, he posits science as the nostrum for all man's ills. Since all knowledge originates in human experience, then the solutions to all physical and psychological problems can be achieved through observation and experimentation in the natural sciences. Every rational concept or theory can be verified or disproved by observation and experimentation. Empiricism negates the role of the soul and free will and reduces man to a super-smart monkey, governed rigidly by the blind forces of nature. Hence, naturalism excludes any knowledge of God or the spiritual world; therefore, it denies that human values as well as moral responsibilities and obligations flow from God. Human conduct is not accountable to God. The naturalist advocates the scientific development of society and scientific, social control. *Brave New World* is a distinctly possible, sequential derivative.

In effect, humanism makes man the central figure in the universe. The ancient Greeks used the word *hubris* to describe this delusion of grandeur. In the Greek tragedies, the protagonist is a person who attains greatness and then loses it because of a "tragic flaw" in his personality that causes his downfall. Some ignoble leaders and officials commit the unpardonable sin of *hubris* as did the protagonist of the ancient Greek dramas. These supreme egotists act as though they are omniscient, omnipotent, and invincible, above the human institutions they preside over, above all reproach.

Hubris is the sin of arrogant pride through which a mere mortal fancies himself equal to the gods. Modern man has nearly attained mastery over the natural forces of his environment but has lost self-control. Science and technology unchecked instill a conscious or subconscious feeling of *hubris* among persons. Wherefore, as in the Greek tragedies, we will be doomed to lose everything, all material wealth, power, prestige, good fellowship and inner peace and tranquility.

Materialism and hedonism are powerful idols of the tribe that hold sway over the minds and bodies of many human beings. The philosophy of materialism leads to glorification of science and technology that strive to harness the natural order. It also incites man to desire material things to satiate all his needs.

Money, lust runs parallel with materialism. Money furnishes access to material wealth. The worship of Mammon is ubiquitous. The spiritual dimension of human experience is squelched or ignored. Ethical behavior, the need for affection and belonging, the esteem, respect, and trust of others, the need for self-discipline, the sublime act of sacrifice for others, these and all other ideals are discarded in man's quest for material objects and physical comfort. The state of mind we call happiness becomes a tormenting illusion.

Hedonism has its origin in materialism. Strip man of his spirituality, and he becomes bestial, pandering to all his base instincts. Hedonism affirms pleasure as the sole good and pain as the sole evil. Hedonists pursue physical pleasure not in moderation, but in excess. They indulge their carnal appetites to surfeit. Life becomes a concatenation of sensations. Morality becomes definable in terms of self-interest; charitableness is forfeit to selfishness. The virtues of prudence, temperance, humility, fortitude, and brotherly love are renounced.

The following modern day parables illustrate the anguish precipitated by the worship of these false gods.

A man and his wife have a combined income of $100,000 from wage earnings. Both husband and wife work and have two children, ages seven and eleven. The parents complain incessantly about not having enough money to live decently. Although they own a fine house in the suburbs, replete with game room and outdoor swimming pool, they bemoan their living conditions. They are dissatisfied with their furniture and their cars, which are no longer new. They want to replace their durable goods with new items; moreover, they want fashionable wardrobes and all the accoutrements of personal adornment. They want to eat out more often at fancy restaurants, travel, and join the country club.

After twelve years of piling up possessions and creature comforts, they are divorced.

A woman is eighty-four years old. She is the mother of three sons and a daughter. She has been a widow for the past ten years. The lady is suffering from debilitating arthritis, which makes it impossible for her to live alone. Her children have contributed monetarily towards her support but are loath to take her into their homes. They profess their love for their mother but agree that it would be best for everyone, especially their mother, if she were institutionalized. They have selected a fine nursing home for her to live in, but she doesn't want to go. Instead, she pleads to be taken in by her children and promises not to make a nuisance of herself. This situation is unresolved until one night the old lady stumbles and falls in the street while doing her marketing. She fractures her pelvis, and, after a three month sojourn in the hospital, she is transferred to a nursing home.

The children visit frequently at first. The mother closes her eyes shortly thereafter.

A seventeen year old youth is marked by dissipation. His face is gaunt and sallow. This young man lives for the moment, grasping at every chance to feel "high." He can't stand sobriety and will do anything for a thrill. Taking drugs has become a way of life to him. To purchase these placebos he resorts to crime. To him nothing is sinful or wrong except self-denial. He is not above lying, stealing and abusing those who love him.

This young man's girl friend is fifteen years old. She also wastes her mind and body with drugs. She prostitutes herself for her boyfriend who claims he loves her. To demonstrate his love he procures men for her and beats her. Of course she has been taking birth control pills to prevent pregnancy. Her obliging mother introduced the contraceptives to her when she was thirteen years old.

This young couple on the threshold of life have vowed to love each other forever and never part. At nineteen years of age the young man dies of an overdose; his beloved, now all of seventeen years, is committed to a sanitarium.

An accountant working for a large corporation is vying with other co-workers for a promotion in the company. The position of department supervisor has become vacant as a result of the dismissal of the alcoholic former supervisor. The ambitious accountant deserves the position on merit and seniority. His past performance has been exemplary. His record of attendance has been excellent. He had rendered yeoman service to his former supervisor, although he never liked him. Everyone in the department expects the accountant to receive the well-paying, managerial position. Another man is awarded the title and salary.

The disgruntled accountant quits his job and finds employment with another company. He becomes contentious with his family and a sycophant to his new boss. He becomes captious with co-workers. He instigates arguments and takes no pleasure in what he does. He harbors hostility towards perfect strangers and denigrates everyone he knows.

Eventually, he becomes one of the millions of malcontented people, unhappy with his lot in life, and unmindful of his blessings.

Saint John Vianney decried false pride. He considered material possessions, honors, etc., as nothingness. He would pity one guilty of *hubris* or obsessed with owning things. A favorite motto of this humble saint was "Sic transit gloria mundi" (Thus passes the glory of the world.) He often compared riches, honors, etc., as grass of the field; it grows and withers anon.

The Second Commandment: *"Thou shalt not take the Lord's name in vain."*

The second commandment proscribes blasphemous or irreverent use of God's name. The ancient Hebrew priests used the name Jehovah or Yaweh sparingly to allude to God. To this day orthodox Jews refrain from direct allusion to God. To these members of the chosen people, the name of God is ineffable, too sacred for utterance.

Christians are on familiar terms with God. We invoke God by name constantly in our liturgies and in private prayers. Doxology, hymns of praise to God, are somewhat popular among Christians. The profound mystery of the Trinity allows a unique opportunity for invoking God in toto or in the particular. We Christians believe that there are three distinct persons in one divine God: the Father, His son Jesus Christ, and the Holy Spirit. Although mysteriously coalesced in a triune God, those persons are discrete beings and are referred to individually.

Jesus spoke of his father as creator and ruler and the Holy Spirit as the one whom He and the Father would send to enlighten and inspire us. We may pray to God as the Blessed Trinity, that is, to the Father through the son in unity with the Holy Spirit. We may pray to any one of the three divine Persons.

The second commandment forbids swearing falsely or flippantly. Our Father's name should not be invoked to asseverate truth in a manner which is not very serious. Imprecations hurled indiscriminately in anger or as a habit are offensive to God. Maledictions mouthed in earnest against someone constitute a grave transgression. To desire harm to betide someone is to court the Evil One. The fallen angels are perpetually on the prowl to prey on the frailty of human beings. When we vent our anger or hatred towards others, we are flouting our Lord's behest to love one another. When we drive love from our hearts, hate and evil will soon fill the void. Without love we become spiritually moribund and highly susceptible to the snares of the devil. When we raise our hearts, thoughts, and voices to God we must do so with the greatest deference and veneration. If we love our Father, we will not profane His name nor take an oath without sufficient reason. In addition, we must never perjure ourselves by calling upon God to witness the truth of something we know to be false. We must never break a vow made in the name of God to do something pleasing to Him.

There is now a disgusting vogue of wearing religious objects such as crosses and medals as personal adornments. Still worse is the display of such items by persons dressed in vulgar or immodest attire. We do not adore our crosses, relics, statues, or holy pictures as objects in themselves. They are images of the God we worship and adore and the saints we honor. There are other fads which are, at least, unwholesome and, at worst, virulent. Clairvoyance, predicting the future, necromancy, and communicating with the dead have piqued the curiosity of many people. There has been an explosion of devilish horror novels and films. In the media, sacred rites and ceremonies of religions are being exploited commercially. What is especially horrifying is that these books and films often depict the Prince of Darkness as a triumphant antagonist, or even a hero. As a result of this trend, there is a growing number of people who have become unduly fearful and even psychologically unbalanced. Some disturbed people are convinced that their houses are haunted or that they are possessed. Finally, this surging fascination with the occult has induced some irreligious and thrill-seeking people to dabble in unholy activities, paving the way to black magic and devil worship.

Two young people are subjected to scurrilous language and swearing by their parents, who are overwrought. They are exposed to other youngsters at school and in the neighborhood who curse and use filthy expletives routinely. Imitating their parents and peers, these children start profaning the Lord's names and uttering obscenities. At this young age they are not guilty of infringing the second commandment as they are oblivious to the evil and rankness of their speech. They are merely parroting what they hear from others. When they start cursing in front of their parents, they are reproached. The children desist from cursing in their parents' presence; skulkingly, they curse and spew filthy words behind their backs. In time, they become habituated to coarse and vulgar language. Reverence for the Lord's name and decent patterns of speech must be instilled at an early age and it is the devoir of the parents of children to set a good example.

There are two sisters who are like night and day. The older sister is ill-favored; the younger sister has outstanding physical beauty. Instead of developing a winsome personality, the older sister is cross and sullen. On the other hand, the younger sister has a genial personality and is simpatico. The homely, older sister is envious of her sister, although the younger sister has arranged double dates which turned into fiascoes because of the nastiness of the older sister. Unwilling to hold down a job, the older sister becomes practically a shut-in. She seldom ventures outside the house and has no social life. The parents of the two sisters are heartsick over their older daughter.

From the depths of her heart, the older sister curses her younger sister with dreadful maledictions. She calls upon God to make her sister unhappy. It comes to pass that the younger sister is courted and married by a fine man whose love is fervent. The older sister feigns gladness, but her envy knows no bounds. She continues to invoke God to make her sister unhappy.

Appealing to God to cause harm or discontent to another person is a noxious sin and will beget vexation to the curser.

Saint John Vianney detested swearing and cursing. He preached against blasphemy for years until its surcease among the townspeople of Ars. He perceived that foul language usually has its roots in the sin of anger. A furious person will blaspheme the holy name of God and accuse His providence. Often the swearing and cursing is triggered by something trivial, a word or even a gesture. A person with a bad temper is predisposed to curse and displays no self-control.

The Third Commandment: *"Remember thou keep holy the Sabbath Day."*

The third commandment adjures us to pay homage to God in a positive, active manner. We are required to devote a specified time to acclaim our faith and love in word and deed. Our Father commands His children to make public acts of tribute and thanksgiving in His honor. God does not make it optional. The Father of Abraham, Isaac, Moses, and Christ decreed a temple to be built in His glory for public worship. He specified the exact construction and mode of worship. Jesus Christ always kept holy the Sabbath day by going to synagogue.

While the first and second commandments tell us what not to do in relation to God, the third commandment clearly orders us to do things pleasing to God. The seven subsequent commandments reveal what God expects of us in our relationship with fellow man. In essence the first three commandments can be fulfilled by loving God; whereas, the seven subsequent commandments can be fulfilled by loving your neighbor as yourself.

Keeping holy the Sabbath obliges the worship of God and the public profession of faith. On Saturday and Sunday all Jews and Christians should congregate in their synagogues and churches to worship God in their special ways.

It is incumbent upon every Jew and Christian to learn all he can about his faith and participate fully in religious observances. Mere physical presence at synagogue and church is not enough. Every Jew and Christian should attend services with his heart uplifted to God. Keeping holy the Sabbath means directing our thoughts and actions to God above everything else.

The person who doesn't frequent synagogue or church and criticizes those who do, calling them hypocrites, is guilty of sitting in judgment of his fellow man. What right does he have to question the motive, or doubt the sincerity, of the church goer? His own negligence and poor example cause as much scandal as those who go through the motions but are not religiously devout. Granted, there are people who go to church and are morally bankrupt while some people who do not go to church are pure of heart. Christ has warned all of us about picking up the first stone. God knows the righteous and the wicked and has marked all of us for the winnowing. A pregnant rhyme comes to mind: "Patrick Murphy went to mass and never missed a Sunday, but Patrick Murphy went to hell for what he did on Monday."

I suspect we become remiss in performance of religious devotions because of a natural inclination to sloth. We become lax when we become lazy. It is easier not to pray and attend services than it is to do so faithfully. Doing the right thing is usually more difficult than doing the wrong thing. Good habits are hard to develop but, surely, are worth the sacrifice. I say these things not to moralize but to reinforce what you already know for fact. Furthermore, we can be quite clever at finding an excuse, a rationalization, for not keeping holy the Sabbath.

A carpenter works six days a week at his trade. On Sundays he spends his time wood-cutting for his pleasure. This man does not attend church services on Sunday, because he does not want to sacrifice his free time. He states that he works hard all week and that he is entitled to a day of leisure. He justifies his labor at wood-cutting as a relaxing pastime. Although his wife desires to attend church services with their young children, he refuses to mind their infant child. She can't manage taking the toddler and two other young children to church by herself. Babysitters don't want to work just for an hour. In effect he is depriving his wife and children from attending church services. This carpenter does not devote any time at all to religious reading or reflections. His wife pleads with him to mend his ways, but he laughs at her. He professes to have religion in his heart. He says that God knows he is a hard-working, clean-living man and will forgive him for not going to church on Sunday.

This carpenter is defiling the Sabbath and is compounding his wrongdoing through rationalization. He will be held accountable to God for his misdeeds. For her part, the wife's intentions are admirable, and she is free of sin.

A wealthy manufacturer has made a fortune through illegal business tactics and exploitation of workers. This white collar thief falsifies his financial statements and defrauds creditors and customers. Inspectors are bribed not to report violations at his factory where working conditions are awful. This man is a prominent member of community and church. On Sundays he struts into church with his family. Although he adulates his wife in front of others, he keeps a mistress. The minister and members of the congregation are eager to ingratiate themselves with him. Of course, he has made tax deductible donations to the church as evidenced by stained glass windows bearing his name.

This man is not a religious person just because he goes to church on Sunday. He does not measure up to God's commandments, especially to love our fellow man, and, therefore, does not keep holy the Sabbath Day.

One of the chief wrongs Saint Vianney sought to rectify when he arrived in Ars was sparse attendance at Sunday mass. He surmised correctly the reason, indifference and indolence. He considered sloth a hydra for other sins. The idle man thinks of eating, drinking, and other ways of pleasuring himself. Hard work is repugnant to him; he would rather indulge his passions. Instead of religious devotions, the men of Ars were preoccupied with dancing and drinking in the early years of Saint Vianney's tenure. The saint would oft warn his parishioners that idleness was the devil's workshop. He quoted the scriptures which threatened: *"My sabbaths ye shall keep: for it is a sign between Me and you throughout your generations. Everyone that defileth it shall surely be put to death."* (Exodus 31:13,14)

CHAPTER EIGHT

Commandments Encompassing
our
Relationship With Others

The Fourth Commandment: *"Thou shalt honor thy father and thy mother."*

During my career as a public school teacher for almost thirty years, I have observed the so-called generation gap existing between young people and their elders widen into a chasm. The alienation and disaffection felt by so many children towards their parents is chilling. Surely there is cause for alarm and corrective action. Why are the youth of today disrespectful, disobedient, and even hostile towards their elders? By virtue of extensive interaction with young people, I have ascertained some of the causes of this execrable state of affairs. The grave spiritual ills that plague our world, irreligion, materialism, selfishness, oppression, immorality, hypocrisy, have warped the psyches of our offspring. Children are not immune to these evils and are losing their innocence at earlier and earlier ages. Children are highly perceptive and suggestible. They learn by imitation and will follow the lead of those closest to themselves. Normally, children are under the aegis of their parents during their young age. The mother, the father, and siblings exert a major influence on a child's character and attitudes. There are diverse elements in the matrix of a child's personality during the formative years from infancy to the age of reason. Family, peers, and teachers play a crucial part in a youngster's personality formation. In addition to satisfying children's physiological needs for adequate food, clothing, and shelter, parents must meet their psychological needs. Children must experience a feeling of belonging and affection, protection from untoward anxieties, discipline and formulation of standards, acquisition of intellectual skills, and a sense of self actualization and esteem.

Children have pressing spiritual needs. Young children are blissfully ignorant of the wicked system of things. Their innocence must be guarded by parents against the interminable assaults of the outside world; assuredly, family life must be held sacrosanct. Parents are responsible for internalizing ideals and high moral standards in their children. Accordingly, they must lead godly, ethical lives for their children to follow suit. They must practice what they preach. How can you presume children will be charitable, honest, industrious, etc., if their parents are not? Parents must earn the love and respect of their sons and daughters by setting a good example.

I believe that large numbers of teenagers are rebellious and fly at authority because they witness the wrongdoing and duplicity of so many adults. These young people are reacting against a system of things fraught with corruption and hypocrisy. They live in a social order that is exploitive, unjust, impersonal, illogical and often brutal. It is no wonder that some teenagers are rejecting organized religion, which is sponsored by the same adults who are responsible for our wicked system of things. To these teenagers, religion is a symbol of the status quo. It is not that they don't believe in God; rather they are searching for God outside organized religion.

In the final analysis, the fathers and mothers of today's children must restore their own credibility. Young people want to see this world as a better place to live. Parents and all adults must win over the hearts and minds of youth by putting their own houses in order. Adults must spearhead amendatory social change. When adults remedy the spiritual ills that plague our world -irreligion, materialism, selfishness, chauvinism, oppression, immorality, and hypocrisy, then they will be honored richly by their children.

A son and a daughter are doted upon by their parents. The children have become accustomed to making demands upon their parents. The parents spoil their children, catering to them. Foolishly, the parents do not distinguish between legitimate need and whim. The children have voracious appetites for material things and are never satisfied; they are showered with expensive clothes, cars, vacations, and jewelry. When the children reach adulthood, they continue to ask for and receive financial support. They welcome the subsidy even though their parents have retired and are living on a fixed income.

This overindulgence on the part of the parents, the greedy leeching of their children, and the gross materialism of all of them, is offensive in the eyes of God.

A man marries a shrew who dislikes his parents. At first he takes a stand against his wife's resentment of his family. They battle verbally and exchange bitter recriminations. She accuses him of being a mama's boy, and he charges she is jealous of his close-knit family. After a while the wife weakens her husband's resistance through guile and stratagem. She pleasures or angers her husband as it suits her, especially in the conjugal bed. There is no living with her unless she has the upper hand. The husband does not have the mettle to subdue her. In time the wife wins him over. He seldom visits his parents for fear of his wife. He absorbs the barrage of criticism of his family by his wife, who barely tolerates them. He begins to resent his own pangs of conscience. In his mind, his family becomes the cause of his marital strife. Eventually, he forswears loyalty to his own family and becomes subject to his wife and in-laws.

This unwarranted disrespect of the wife towards her husband's family and the lack of filial love for his parents on the part of the son are serious sins in the eyes of God.

Saint Vianney loved his parents dearly. He loved children with a great love as evinced in the establishment of *La Providence*. Saint Vianney would be sympathetic towards the youth of today. Who is responsible for the malignancies of war, genocide, drugs, divorce, social injustice, pornography, etc.? Adults, not children. Who is responsible for the deleterious, false values choking our society? Adults, not children. Saint Vianney never accused the children of Ars of vice or not honoring their parents. Rather, he chided unfit parents for setting a bad example for their children. Without a doubt, he would assail adults today for victimizing children.

The Fifth Commandment: *"Thou shalt not kill."*

By this commandment we are forbidden to commit murder, abortion, euthanasia, suicide, mutilation of our body, risking our life without sufficient reason, impairing our health, and maltreating others.

No one but God creates life; no one but God should extinguish life. Murder is the deliberate and needless termination of human life. Deliberation denotes sanity and volition during the act of killing. Although he commits a heinous crime, a person in a blind rage who kills someone is not guilty of murder in the strict sense of the word. How can such a killing be deliberate, that is, willful, if the killer is irrational at the time he does it? He cannot reflect on what he is doing while he is doing it.

To kill in self-defense is not murder if the killing is absolutely necessary to preserve your own life. But there must be a clear and present danger to your life with no alternative but to slay your assailant. Abortion is murder since a fetus is a human life from the moment of conception. Regardless of circumstances, euthanasia is murder since it is the deliberate and unnecessary taking of life.

Killing others in military combat can be murder since most wars are neither just nor justifiable. Unless subject to direct military attack and aggression and for reason of self-defense, we should be pacifists and military objectors. Suicide is tantamount to self-murder since it is the deliberate and unnecessary taking of one's own life. A person is a steward of the gift of life. God entrusts this life to us for our safekeeping during our appointed time on earth. We are obliged to use every ordinary means to preserve human life and health. To vitiate one's health through intemperate living is inexcusable. Gluttony and overindulgence in the use of alcohol and tobacco are hazardous to one's health and therefore against the fifth commandment.

To intentionally harm or demean other people is odious in the eyes of God. To hate others is contrary to God's will. In the Bible we are taught to bless, not curse, our enemies. Religious and racial bigotry, wishing evil on others, refusing to forgive trespasses against us, and seeking revenge are all sins against the fifth commandment. The antithesis of hatred is love. Keeping the fifth commandment compels much more than not hating or hurting others. We must not be callous toward our brothers and sisters but must love them wholeheartedly and help them unstintingly. Love fires a genuine concern and interest in our fellow man, a need to be close to him. Universal love and brotherhood can blossom and propagate through the interdependence of all peoples. God is love and love is the seed and sustenance of life, the awesome power which creates the seasons and constellations in undying cycles. The spirit of the universe is one and that spirit is love.

Millions of men, women, and children die of starvation or malnutrition every year. Drought and pestilence kill millions in underdeveloped countries, particularly in Asia and Africa. Incalculable impoverished families do not have enough clothes or decent housing. Inhabiting squalid warrens where disease and crime proliferate, they are denied adequate health care, police and fire protection, and good schools for their children. There are many hapless souls confined in institutions, forsaken by their families and people they know. The elderly and infirm, the chronically ill, the retarded and mentally disturbed, the incarcerated, these people languish day after day waiting for visitors. Masses of people are uneducated and unskilled with dim prospects for job training and employment. Ever so many people are troubled and disconsolate. They suffer from terrible misfortune of their own making or beyond their control. Many are afflicted with the malaise sweeping our world.

Charity is the giving of oneself rather than the offering of some object. Aloof and perfunctory almsgiving is not charity but balm for our conscience. Such almsgiving does not discharge our moral obligation to share our blessings with those in need. True charity is to share our time, talents, and material possessions with all members of the human family. How do we express our love for our fellow man? We express fraternal love through a deep and abiding reverence for life. Commitment to improve the human condition and enhance the quality of all people is the *sine qua non*. Performance of good deeds, not mawkish sentimentality, spells love in action. We should not feel bound by conscience but rather privileged to perform the works of mercy. At every opportunity we should feed the hungry, give drink to the thirsty, clothe the naked, shelter the homeless, visit those who are sick, lonely, or imprisoned, bury the dead, convert the sinner, instruct the ignorant, counsel the doubtful, comfort the sorrowful, bear wrongs patiently, forgive injuries, and pray for the living and the dead.

Not until every person becomes his brother's keeper and tends to the spiritual and temporal welfare of all others can we hope for a better world. A spiritual resurrection of man is prerequisite. We must slough off our egotism and be prepossessed to love. We must no longer turn our backs to each other but cleave to each other as spiritual kin. We must make time in our busy lives to assist the less fortunate. Our good works should be performed not with fanfare but with quiet humility. True altruism rules out self-aggrandizement. We can volunteer our services to hospitals, nursing homes, community centers and charitable foundations. We can contribute a fixed percentage of our income to charitable and non-profit organizations. Of course, this entails personal sacrifice, the surrender of something for the sake of someone else. A desideratum is an unselfish concern that freely accepts others as equals and seeks their good.

A fifteen-year old girl becomes pregnant by her

sixteen-year- old boyfriend. This fact is confirmed by a doctor in the girl's second month of being with child. These two people are not in a position to get married and start a family. They do not have the self-discipline, maturity or love for a successful marriage. The young man is unwilling to take on the weighty responsibilities of marriage and fatherhood as he wishes to concentrate on his education and prepare for a profession. He tries desperately to persuade his girlfriend to have an abortion. The parents of the girl demand that she has an abortion. They are sure that having a child will hinder her future.

The girl's emotions are awry. She is uncertain of her feelings for her boyfriend and admits that he is not suited for fatherhood at this time. Yet, she wants fervidly to have this baby. She is confident that she will love this child always and be a good mother. The alternative of adoption is given consideration, but the girl determines that she cannot bear the child and then part with it. Her life becomes a nightmare. The parents become accusatory towards her and adamantly insist upon an abortion. The young man resists betrothal and then deserts her. In the fifth month of healthy life, the baby is murdered.

Is not this abortion a violation of the natural law and a grave sin in the eyes of God?

A child is born in the ghetto. The mother has borne this baby boy to increase her welfare payments. The father is unknown and is one of her legion of lovers. As a child he is pummeled, not caressed, by his mother, who is often drunk. His home is a noisome, unheated, rat-infested, tenement flat. His body and mind are constricted by malnutrition and neglect.

No one cares about him and no one listens to him. He becomes taciturn, withdrawn, and angry with the world. He relishes the idea of becoming an arch enemy of a society that condones his plight. The street becomes his educator. Quite intelligent, he quickly learns the ways of a jungle prowled by degenerates and criminals. Dope pushers provide respite from reality. As a teenager he shoplifts from stores, steals cars, and mugs people. Shortly after his eighteenth birthday, he murders a policeman in a shoot-out while attempting to rob a store. Capital punishment is allowed in his state. He is brought to trial, found guilty of murder, and sentenced to death.

Is not society guilty of the spiritual homicide of this criminal? Will killing him restore the life of the policeman or allay the grief of his family? Is this person beyond all hope of rehabilitation and doing some good with his life? Would not life incarceration be enough retributive suffering? Aren't capital punishment and the fifth commandment really incompatible?

Saint Vianney identified anger as the mainspring of murder. This emotion, he made known explicitly, comes from the devil. Anger shows that the devil is in control of our heart and can inflame our passions. We are like puppets in his hands; the old saw, "the devil made me do it", has more than a smidgin of truth to it. Saint Vianney compared an enraged person to a bristling hedgehog, a scorpion, and a furious lion. He advises that we be mindful of our guardian angel who is always at our side. In so doing we would be ashamed to fly into a rage. When anger reaches the point of wanting to kill someone, it is a sin against the fifth commandment. Jesus Christ put us on guard to be wary of this sin: *"Everyone who is angry with his brother shall be liable to judgment."* (Matthew 5:22)

The Sixth Commandment: *"Thou shalt not commit adultery."*
The Ninth Commandment: *"Thou shalt not covet the neighbor's wife."*

The sixth and ninth commandments are especially difficult to uphold. Infractions of other commandments involve intellect and will. Sins against purity encompass intellect, will and potent body chemistry. Our biological urges, coupled with society's sexual license, make self-control almost impossible at times. Decadence all around us militates against rectitude, especially chastity. Our visceral appetite to have sexual intercourse is objectively
good and necessary. If we didn't desire sex, the survival of our species would be endangered. It is the misuse of our sex faculties that is evil and causes people great consternation.

First and foremost, a distinction must be made between sexual desire and erotic love. The cause of sexual desire is the mounting of libidinal energy which periodically builds tension within us. Release can be accomplished with or without physical fusion. The fulfillment of erotic love is decidedly more complex. It demands the sharing of mind and soul as well as body. Erotic love can be consummated only by the union of a man and woman who have committed their lives to each other. Such a commitment relies on the intellect to make value judgments about one another and an act of the will to endure.

The art of loving, what love is, and its place among married and single couples, has been the subject of exhaustive research and analysis by countless experts in many disciplines. There is no doubt in my mind that love is indeed the magic ingredient that makes the world go round. What, however, is conductive to love is surely a matter of speculation. Our media of communication have cast a strong spell over our populace. Movies, television, radio, records, books, and magazines have lulled us into a hypnagogic state. We have been mesmerized and entranced by the pipe-dream, story-book approach toward love. We ingest and digest this romantic drivel ad nauseam. After a period of time, our minds, beleaguered bastions of reason, cave in to the endless siege and we caress the simulacrum that we have fallen in love.

Sex is an operation of the body, a material substance, while love is an operation of the intellect and will, which comprise the spiritual substance of the soul. Sex is the means through which the demands of the id are satisfied. The formal object of sex is procreation, while the material object is pleasure. The formal object of the intellect is the attainment of truth, while the material object is the logical operation of the mind. Truth is knowledge, that is, when we know something as it exists in reality, then we have a certain knowledge of that something. Truth, or knowledge, is the conformity of our thoughts with objective reality. When we say that we love another person, we imply that our thoughts about the person agree with the truth. The body of another person appeals to my senses. Thus, the sight and touch of that person produces all sorts of pleasurable sensations in me. By the same token, another person's mind and personality appeal to me. I come to know, then to love, that person through the operation of my intellect: through ideas, judgments, and inferences about that person. I can express my love for that person by being kind and considerate, responsive to his or her needs, and by eliciting the very best qualities of that person.

Sex and love are separate and distinct entities. Although they can be enjoyed separately, they are complementary. When coalesced through a long-lasting marriage, they become hard to distinguish. A parlous deficiency affects many marriages today. People are feasting their bodies and starving their souls. More and more people are mistaking sexual desire for love. They are attracted to each other by physical attributes and the desire for intimacy and enter ill-conceived marriages. With the passing of time, their amatory ardor wanes. Their intellectual compatibility, behavioral and emotional tendencies, personal and social traits, attitudes, and habits take on an overriding importance. When these features come into conflict, abrasive arguments and strained relationships ensue. All too often, spouses conclude that they are mismatched and wind up in divorce court.

Adultery strikes at the very heart of marriage vows. When a man pledges his troth to a woman in marriage, he conjoins with her in spirit. To philander is to abrogate a sacred trust. Adultery wrecks marriages. The husband and the wife are the nucleus of the family. When they are unfaithful to each other, they can be disloyal to everyone else, including their own children. Adultery often brings on divorce and the children become the innocent victims of a broken home. Even when the marriage is not terminated, the stability and cohesiveness of family life is impaired. The fact that married couples are sometimes physically attracted to, and desirous of, others is unavoidable. But to deliberately seek such arousal is perfidious. Husbands and wives should take every precaution against infidelity. This means cultivating a wholesome modesty in speech, manners, and dress; also avoiding occasions of temptation like wild parties and being away from your spouse for long periods of time. Married persons should have friends who are upright and trustworthy.

Marital discord embroils all the members of the family in vitriolic disputes and hard feelings. Restoration of peace through honest dialogue and corrective measures is imperative. Spouses should be fair-minded, seeing each other's valid points. Consortium is the marriage right of one spouse to the company and affection of the other. Refusal of the marriage rights, specifically sexual intercourse, to win a quarrel is shameful. No effort should be spared to preserve the marriage union. Every reasonable measure should be taken to effect reconciliation. However, there are breaches of the wedding vows such as alcoholism and drug addiction, criminal activity, adultery, unremitting gambling, nonsupport, and acts of violence which may prove insuperable and justify temporary, and even permanent, separation.

Fornication and cohabitating couples make up a moral decay sweeping our permissive society. Sex outside of marriage is so commonplace as to constitute the norm. Even many parents do not disapprove of this immorality on the part of their sons and daughters. Virginity is not only not prized, it is ridiculed by many young people who think being pure is droll. So-called role models, especially in entertainment, have made a mockery of chastity. Immorality is the cause of the pandemic of venereal disease and AIDS. Sexual promiscuity contravenes the basis of marriage. So many people today are glutting their sensuality without assuming the responsibilities of the married state. What incentive do they have to get married? And if they do wed, what chance is there for a lasting marriage? People have acquired voracious appetites for sex without developing meaningful relationships. Men and women are engaging in sexual relations without even knowing each other, often during a first encounter. How can the sex act become a fulfilling expression of love if, and when, they marry? How can coition strengthen the connubial ties that join them together? How can they be satisfied sexually with one person after sleeping with many others? Promiscuous sex corrodes the moral fiber of a person. He or she tends to see other people as sex objects not human beings. This distorted view completely ignores the psychological and emotional aspects of sexual relations and is, in fact, dehumanizing.

Those young people who do remain chaste before marriage show maturity and wisdom. Through self-restraint they gird themselves not only for the obligations and discipline of married life but also for the rigors and hardships of life in general. Chaste people exercise great care to avoid sexual stimulation or compromising situations. They are usually religious and active in their church where there are opportunities to meet like-minded individuals. Unless they are in a position to contemplate marriage, they will not consent to steady company-keeping or engagement. They appreciate that frequent, exclusive dating creates an overpowering desire for sex and will hasten intimacy. When a chaste young couple decide to tie the nuptial bonds, they don't wait a long time to do so.

One of the most invidious sources of moral degeneration is the staggering amount of pornographic materials, including books, magazines, videos, and films now mass-produced for public consumption. It is sickening to behold the innumerable obscene publications and films that have been disseminated throughout the world. Pornography is polluting the minds of children as well as adults. Young boys and girls are exposed to an amassment of adult magazines every time they buy a comic book or pack of chewing gum. The adolescent is particularly vulnerable because he is itching to satisfy an understandable curiosity about sex and is experiencing puberty. Although youngsters cannot legally buy pornography, such magazines and videos quickly wind up in the hands of children. Older friends purchase them and pass them around. Discarded issues and tapes are everywhere. We are figuratively drowning in a sea of scatology. It is an outrage that our society will permit the natural sexual awakening of young people to be exploited and corrupted.

I am sure there are millions of people who are incensed over this flood of filth. Decent people must combat the pornographers with every legal means at our disposal. For too long these panderers have sabotaged the purport of our constitutional right of freedom of expression. For too long our courts have allowed license to supplant liberty. Consequently, books, magazines, and video exhibiting explicit sexual acts of copulation, fellatio, cunnilingus, bestiality, and even sex between adults and children are available everywhere. It is not enough to wring our hands or to mouth disapproval among ourselves. People must battle to end the upsurge of pornography once and for all. We must coordinate a massive letter writing campaign to legislators, government officials, and judges. We have the clout to make pornography a legal issue, and extend support for all proposed legislation banning or restricting pornography. There are a number of fine organizations combatting pornography that we can support. All lawful tactics must be brought to bear to abolish pornography.

Buddhist and Hindu philosophy postulate that desire is the fountainhead of much human misery; that through the cessation of desire we are able to realize serenity and peace of heart. Through relinquishment of our desires to gain power and prestige, to make a lot of money, to accumulate material possessions, to placate the propensities of our lower nature toward selfishness, indolence, lust, gluttony, envy, and anger, we are able to contemplate and concentrate on knowing, loving, and serving God. We may be endowed with many blessings: good health, a rewarding occupation, a loving family, respect of other people, and the material goods of the world. But we cannot be happy if we are not close to God.

Sin is the willful disobedience of a law of God. If one has the intent to commit a sin, but for some reason cannot carry out the offense, he is still guilty of transgression in the eyes of God. The consequences of sin are that we offend God, and there is a diminution of our ability to resist further temptation to sin. Sin blocks our path to God. Because of their willful disobedience, our forbears were banished from the garden of Eden and were punished severely. The angels have cause to hate and be jealous of us. When they rebelled against God, they were cast into hell. When we rebelled against God through Adam and Eve, we were promised a redeemer. We disobey the will of God when we sin. We circumvent our own will when we sin, because our will is to do what is good for oneself. Whenever we do something bad, there is always some apparent good. People steal, lie, and philander because they believe mistakenly these acts are in their best interests; that by doing these things some greater good will redound to them. This accounts for the attractiveness of turpitude and the temptation it poses. Sinful habits must be overcome and occasions of sin avoided. You cannot expect to mire yourself in a sinful ambience and remain unsullied.

Temptation is any enticement that induces us to

sin. Temptations emanate from the devil and the evil designs of other people. When we are tempted, we must pray to God for help to overcome the temptation. Self-discipline is good for the soul as well as the body. By denying ourselves, from time to time, the small, innocuous pleasures, the snack between meals, the second cup of coffee, the television sports special, we fortify ourselves against the impulse to sin. Mortification of the flesh through penance and fasting will tame passions and bolster our willpower not to sin. If we cater to every whim, we will capitulate to every temptation and end up a libertine.

God is all merciful and will never withhold forgiveness for our sins, no matter how serious, if we are truly repentant and resolved not to sin again. Saint Vianney told penitents that their sins were like a speck of dirt next to the mountain of God's mercy. Whereas God's justice calls for personal penance, Jesus Christ has atoned for all our sins, it is crucial that we turn to God and away from sin. Instead of lusting after things of the world, we must center our interest on God and keeping His commandments.

A teenage girl is overcome by the sex mania fixating our society. She rabidly reads all the lust novels on the best seller lists and talks about them with her girlfriends. Together with her girlfriends she ogles nude male anatomies in magazines and movies. Her friends and she exchange information on the mechanics of sexual relations and methods of contraception. They have been saturated with instruction about having "safe sex" at their local high school, where condoms are readily distributed upon request. Most of her girlfriends are having sex with their ever-changing boyfriends. They give her glowing accounts of the joys of orgasm.

At the tender age of fourteen, this sophisticated maiden has herself deflowered on the back seat of a car.

In her coed dorm at college a young woman considers herself liberated and sexually favors all sorts of men. Upon graduation, she moves into an apartment in the city and flings herself into the swinging singles' scene. At thirty-five years of age her face is sodden from continuous indulgence in loose living. She cannot remember the names or faces of all the men with whom she has coupled. One man after another lives with her, but, strange as it may seem, none of them will marry her.

This pathetic woman does not realize that defying the sixth commandment not only offends God but also harms the offender in divers ways.

Saint Vianney considered the sin of lust the most difficult to overcome. The devils who tempt us to commit this sin do not commit it themselves. Those who are hardened in impurity are like a piece of cloth stained with oil; it is very difficult to eradicate. Saint Vianney reminds us that our bodies are temples of the Holy Spirit, the Spirit cannot dwell in us if we are all flesh and corruption. Even in old age, when the passions have subsided, men entertain memories and thoughts of debauchery. As predicted in the New Testament, men and women in these last days are no longer ashamed of being impure; rather they boast of it and recruit others to join them. They have faces of brass and hearts of bronze, closing their ears to any talk of virtue.

The Seventh Commandment: *"Thou shalt not steal."*
The Tenth Commandment: *"Thou shalt not covet*

they neighbor's goods."

These commandments govern the possession and use of property. The right to private property is not a birthright based on natural law. All material things belong to the Lord and are gifts to all men. God has given man dominion over the creatures and things of the earth for his collective good. Therefore, no one has the moral right to usurp material things for himself to the detriment of his fellow man. It follows, then, that stewardship does not entitle a person to profligacy in the use of material goods. No one has the right to do whatever he pleases with property since all things were created to serve the common good. In fact, it is a binding duty of property stewards to share with others who lack material needs through no fault of their own. I use the word *steward* advisedly. I don't believe man has an inalienable right to own things. We come into the world with no earthly goods, and we leave with none. Proprietorship is a convention of society. But the precepts of every society ordain that, although a person has a legal title to something, his possession is never absolute but conditional. Stewardship connotes the management of things God has entrusted to us and others. The concept of *caritas* or caring for others is interwoven throughout the commandments of God. All human rights give rise to corresponding obligations. We have the right to furnish ourselves with necessities and reasonable comforts. This right exacts the corresponding obligation to share superfluous goods with people who hardly have the basic necessities of life.

Jesus Christ was born in relative poverty and led an simple life. He cautioned his followers to shun earthly riches that distract and deter people from keeping the commandments of God. Jesus said to his disciples, *"I assure you, only with difficulty will a rich man enter into the kingdom of God."* (Matthew 19:23). This does not mean wealth is intrinsically evil, but tends to endear us to materialism, preoccupying our minds and crowding out notions of discipline and sacrifice. Wealth tends to make the human will soft and flaccid, which is not consonant with keeping the commandments. Then, again, wealth can be used to improve the lot of the poor and needy. The Bible sings praises of personages who were wealthy and honorable. Christ's life was the way of the cross, and poverty was part of His crucible to redeem mankind. A dearth of material things may pave the road to sainthood for some and hell for others. Grinding poverty is no blessing. It makes a person self-contemptuous and hateful of society. What is a correct attitude toward earthly riches? We should not be desirous of wealth, but be provident about our temporal welfare, and husband our material resources.

Critics of organized religion hurl invectives against the churches for having money and property. They claim that religious denominations are disgustingly rich, always beseeching more money; also, that clergymen live in affluence and are insensitive to the poverty-stricken. The Catholic Church, especially the Vatican, is often targeted for vituperation. It is true that organized religion has property, churches, synagogues, hospitals, nursing homes, schools, etc. - but these institutions are built and maintained not to benefit the clergy but to do good for people. The Vatican's art treasurers are open to the whole world. Their beauty appeals to the aesthetic spirit of all people. The art treasures are described as priceless not in terms of money but as sources of euphoria and inspiration to rich and poor alike. Who can visit St. Peter's Basilica without being transfixed in awe and admiration for man's uplifting and ennobling creativity?

Financially, organized religions are fighting for survival. Many churches are deep in debt and must raise more money each year to defray their operating expenses. Without the donations of their congregations, churches would be incapable to do all the good work God commands. Anyone who does not recognize the financial straits of our churches and fails to see their need for contributions to function, is either an inveterate foe or fool.

Missionaries in underdeveloped countries labor to lessen the deprivation of their people. Missionaries know full well you can't preach religion to people who are hungry. Until these people can throw off the yoke of abject poverty, the best of sermons will fall on deaf ears. Such indigence stunts the bodies and minds of these people and crushes their spirit. The answer does not lie in an unending hand out. The answer lies in helping these people achieve self-sufficiency and dignity. Clergymen in impoverished areas have become social agitators. They do not immure themselves behind the walls of their churches, but are out in the streets with the people. They seek better nutrition, housing, community facilities, educational and vocational training, and job opportunities for their needy flocks. Furthermore, priests, ministers, and rabbis have become active in civic affairs, even politics, to eliminate the causes of poverty and bring about social change.

We comply with the seventh and tenth commandments by not damaging or destroying the property of others, by doing business honestly, by honoring our just debts and contracts, by doing an honest day's work for our employers and paying a decent wage to our employees, and by returning or attempting to return lost or stolen goods to their rightful stewards. When we cannot return money or goods we have stolen to their rightful stewards, we must make restitution to them. We should never keep stolen property. When we cannot locate the rightful stewards, we should donate the money or goods to charity.

We breach the seventh and tenth commandments by purloining what belongs to others, by engaging in fraud, cheating, bribery or graft, by profiteering through exorbitant prices in goods we sell or interest charges on loans we make, by deliberately selling spoiled or defective goods or otherwise taking advantage of others in business dealings, and by enviously desiring another's possessions.

Governments of rich and poor nations throughout the world drain their working classes of earned income via taxation in order to spend stupendous sums of money for military operations and superfluous civilian programs that benefit wealthy special interest groups but not the general public. The expenditures for military personnel, bases, and ordnance often devour most of the national budget. These military allocations are usually far in excess of what is necessary for self-defense and greatly intensify world tension. In 1995, the U.S. Congress appropriated seven billion dollars *more* than the Pentagon had requisitioned for its annual budget! Arms stockpiling exacerbates the chances of an outbreak of war among unfriendly nations.

Unproductive military goods and services do not abet the public welfare. Insufficient monies are doled out to social services that enhance the quality of life such as medical research and anti-poverty programs. Disbursements for governmental administration and bureaucratic agencies are mind-boggling. Corruption and waste are rife, and many of the functionaries employed are inefficient or incompetent. These people are appointed to their sinecures through political patronage and nepotism. Advancement through the ranks of civil service often depends on deals and connections rather than merit. So-called public servants in high office reap extravagant salaries and fringe benefits. They do little or no work but delegate responsibilities to their subordinates.

In effect, the hardworking taxpayers are being hoodwinked and robbed. The gross misappropriation and prodigal spending of tax money is tantamount to fraud and theft of service.

Our welfare system is a disgrace! Industrious, middle-class people are taking the brunt of ravaging taxation. The welfare recipients pay hardly any taxes and are parasites living off the productivity of the working class. They don't know the meaning of manual labor, have no scruples, and are the dregs of society. Ironically, I am describing the upper class.

The rich and powerful don't pay their fair share of taxes. The tax laws are written and legislated by their minions, the politicians. A labyrinth of loopholes enables them to retain almost all of their income. They enjoy all the social services the government provides without shouldering their share of cost. The wealthy set up philanthropies administered by toadies who do their bidding and whose large salaries deplete the operating budgets. Of course, the largesse of the patricians is deductible.

In effect, our tax structure shelters the rich and has created a welfare class of wealthy at the expense of the working class.

Saint Vianney recoiled from the sin of avarice from which spring stealing and covetousness. The inordinate pursuit of the goods of this world makes us forget prayer, the sacraments, even God. Wealth and possessions become a false god to the avaricious person. He is not above theft and defrauding others to amass wealth; the avaricious man lives in torment, knowing that he must die and leave all his ill-gotten wealth to others. Good Christians do not become obsessed with the goods of the world; they are not greedy and rapacious. While they are on earth their eyes are fixed on heaven, not a worldly fortune.

The Eighth Commandment: *"Thou shalt not bear false witness against thy neighbor."*

What is truth? How can I apprehend truth? Should I seek truth? Does knowledge of truth lead to happiness or misery, good or evil? Does knowledge of the truth make me free? Do I know the truth about myself? Who am I?

We search for these answers all the days of our life. These thoughts appertain to the very essence of our being, the purpose of our existence. When we seriously seek the truth we must turn to God. Jesus Christ said, *"I am the truth, and the life."* (John 14:6) The word of God is truth. We learn truth through diligent study of the sacred scriptures and the tenets of our religion. We have God's assurance that earnest pursuit of His truth will be rewarded with eternal life. Through the discipline of living a moral life we smash the fetters of sinfulness and are freed from the ranting claptrap of a dissolute world. Remember, there is freedom only in discipline. God's truth is everywhere and ever the same. Persons of faith can exult in the truth that we are children of God created to know, love, and serve Him and fellow man and share eternal happiness with Him in heaven.

What is a lie? A lie is the non-conformity of our thought with our speech. We may say something that is untrue and not lie. At the time, we believe what we say to be the truth. Therefore, there is no intent to deceive the listener. Psychologically, lying is a defense mechanism to relieve inner anxieties by protecting us from a disagreeable truth through deliberate distortion or hiding the truth from others. When we falsify what we believe to be true, we conceal the fact that we have ulterior motives. Often we project onto others motives or thoughts of our own that cause us anxiety. Other people become the target of aggressiveness we might have turned against ourselves. Rationalization is a way of allaying anxieties by denying that we are frustrated or guilty of some wrongdoing. Rationalization amounts to lying to ourselves. Lying is an affront to the human intellect. Through the oral and written word we communicate our thoughts and thinking in an operation of the intellect. We frustrate the natural law when we don't communicate what we are thinking. By extension, this applies to non-verbal communication, signs, gestures, facial expressions, etc., as well.

There is a sanctity in language which is inviolable. Language is the cornerstone of mutual understanding and trust. To prevaricate is to betray man's social nature. Civilization could not exist without mutual trust and faith among men, and trust cannot be established without truthful language. I believe one of the reasons for global tensions is the dissolution of honest communication among people, leading to hypocrisy, dissimulation, equivocation, misrepresentation, and diffusion of propaganda.

These evasions of truth cause distrust, fearfulness, rancor, and fighting among people. Lying is intrinsically evil. There is no such thing as a white lie. There are circumstances which justify the telling of a lie as the lesser of two evils. Preservation of innocent life, avoidance of anguish and injury, and safeguarding the common good are defensible reasons to lie. Ordinarily, to rebut a lie with another lie is to compound a wrongdoing. When someone tells a lie, and we know this to be the case, we are bound in good conscience to speak the truth.

The eighth commandment forbids calumny and detraction . Calumny is the circulation of untruths about a person, calculated to tarnish his or her reputation. Detraction is the unnecessary revelations of faults and misdeeds of a person, again to damage his or her reputation. We are never allowed to scandalize another person unless the common good requires the revelation of the truth. We are obliged to divulge unsavory truths in order to protect innocent persons and bring miscreants to justice. A person guilty of calumny or detraction must try to restore the good name and make restitution for any loss or damage sustained by the person who has been slurred.

A teenage boy has little scholastic aptitude or liking for school. Instead he is dexterous with his hands and adroit at woodcutting. He desires a vocational education to prepare him for the trade of a carpenter. However, his parents object to his working with his hands for a living and press him to go to college. They cajole him with a large allowance and buy him whatever he desires. The parents tell their son he will make them very proud if he goes to college but will break their heart if he doesn't. After conferring with the parents, the boy's high school counselor urges the boy to go to college. In his complicity the counselor exaggerates the boy's potential for college studies. The boy is convinced, and his mind is made up to go to college. Subsequently, he is graduated from high school with minimal grades and is finally accepted into a distant, private college. He flounders for two frustrating years with neither the ability nor the desire for his studies. He drops out before he is expelled.

Are not the elders of this young man guilty of twisting the truth? Have they not worked a great hardship on the young man to no avail? Did they not do him a disservice and an injustice?

A young woman comes to love a young man who wheedles her into having sex with him before marriage. After seducing this callow girl, he abandons her. In time he makes sport of her to his friends. Furthermore, the so-called friends of the woman learn of her predicament. They, in turn, gossip and spread the story behind her back causing woe to her and bringing disgrace upon the woman and her family.

Is not this slander offensive to God and all decent people? Should these calumniators defame the woman with impunity? Shouldn't her family and friends rally to her defense?

Saint Vianney believed that envious people invent all sorts of wickedness against their neighbor. In order to blacken their neighbor they have recourse to lies, calumny, and evil speaking. The envious person feels sadness at the happiness or good fortune of others. Therefore, the jealous person seeks to destroy others through malicious falsehoods. Good Christians love their neighbor and rejoice when good things happen to them. They never commit the sin of envy and never speak evil or falsely of others. The sin of envy comes from hell. The devils envy us because we can attain the glory and bliss of heaven. Satan despised Saint vianney because he was so close to God.

CHAPTER NINE

Are These The Last Days?

The decadence extent in Europe and America parallels that of the Roman Empire preceding its downfall. The symptoms of decline are the same. Large numbers of people have deserted the countryside to dwell in the cities. Masses of people subsist on government doles. Our jaded populace has become lustful and violent, craving entertainment that is lewd and bloody spectacle. Adultery, fornication, homosexuality, pornography, divorce, and abortion have become commonplace. Envy, thievery, greed, gluttony, sloth, intemperance and imprudence have become a way of life for many people. A segment of our youth are alienated, unruly and already dissipated. Crime is soaring (over one million Americans are in jail), and justice is often a purchased commodity.

It is exceedingly possible that we are now living in the last days, the final epoch before the end of this world order. The portents foretold by Jesus Christ seem clearly visible. Cataclysms such as earthquakes, floods, and famine are occurring with increased frequency. False prophets are everywhere using the guise of religion to mask their reprehensible objectives. Many of our leading figures are corrupt, immoral, and power-mad. Our world has become a cloaca, an environmental and moral cesspool. We have despoiled the atmosphere, the oceans, and terrain almost beyond redemption. We are living in a spiritual wasteland. Can you pick up a newspaper without reading about crime, violence, and scandal? Can you enter a stationery store without being faced by a plethora of pornographic magazines? Do you not see the flood of lascivious, violent books and movies to debase you and your children? Are you not aware that the sanctuary of your home is being invaded by the devil through the medium of television? Programs are permeated with sex, violence, and mockery of religion and sacred beliefs. In his hard-hitting book, *Hollywood vs. America*, Michael Medved chronicles the entertainment industry's attack on traditional family values and religion, its addiction to sex and violence, and the monstrous impact of these assaults on our society and children. In the award-winning videos *Marian Apparitions of the 20th Century* and *Time for Mercy* produced by Marian Communications in Lima, Pennsylvania, the apparitions of the Blessed Mother are presented with her message of urgency for all mankind. Our Blessed Mother has appeared around the world: Fatima, Portugal; Banneux and Beauraing, Belgium; Zeitum, Egypt; Garabandal, Spain; Akita, Japan; Betania, Venezuela; Medjugorje, Yugoslavia; Kibeho, Rwanda (Africa); Naju, Korea; and the Soviet Union. Always her message is the same to the visionaries: we are on the brink of destruction with a coming chastisement for the entire world unless we repent, pray, fast, and convert our lives to God and away from sin. Let us be mindful that divine retribution for iniquity is evidenced in the Bible in the decimation of mankind in the great flood of Noah's time and the destruction of Sodom and Gomorrah. Modern skeptics should remember the incredible comet which struck Jupiter in 1993. Had this unforseen comet hit the earth, instead of Jupiter, numberless people would have been wiped out.

Newspaper accounts at the time reported that astronomers estimate that thousands of comets are speeding through space in paths that cross the earth's orbit and are big enough to do global damage. In his book, *Catholic Prophecy*, Yves Dupont details prophecies of a coming comet which will soon strike the earth if people will not mend their ways. This exceptional occurrence will be permitted by God as a punishment for the sins of man.

In the end time, the devils will be on a rampage. Aware that there is only a short time left before the Second Coming of Christ and the Last Judgement, they are capturing as many souls as possible before they are cast back into hell forevermore. Bible prophecies portending the Second Coming of Christ have been fulfilled in our time. The establishment of the State of Israel in 1948 marks the permanent return of the Jews to their homeland after the great Diaspora, the dispersion of Jews throughout the world during the Roman occupation. Another momentous prophecy which has been fulfilled in our lifetime is the restoration of Jerusalem to the Jews. In 1967 the Gentiles, i.e., foreign powers, were driven out of Jerusalem, thus fulfilling the inspired prediction, *"Jerusalem shall be trodden down by the Gentiles till the times of the nations be fulfilled."* (Luke 21:24). Scriptures foretell the ascent of the demoniac Anti-Christ prefacing the Second Coming of Christ. This great antagonist will fill the world with wickedness and tribulations but will be conquered forever by Christ at His Second Coming. The Anti-Christ may be the personification of evil taking the form of a despot who will reign over the entire world or the Anti-Christ may be a term used to describe a wicked system of things such as we have today. During the hegemony of the Anti-Christ, people will turn to God and abide by His commandments or else, utterly reject God and religion. Again, this seems to be the scenario we are experiencing today with people worshipping the true God or false gods they have fashioned themselves.

Retrenchment is the guidework for the religious person today. It has become nearly impossible to avoid temptation and escape corruption in this pagan world. Religious persons must band together and draw from each other's strength. However, we must not become religious recluses, sequestered from the world, for it is incumbent upon us to convert sinners. Although we are beset with formidable temptations, we can develop the mettle to resist them. Active participation in church affairs, spiritual retreats, daily Bible reading, and prayer are essential for the faithful. A person who walks with God radiates optimism in a cynical world. Such a person is infused with faith and trust in God's protection against all evildoers. His and her life is not frenetic but peaceful. A patina of love and goodness illumines the face of a child of God. A child of God does not fear death, for death is the portal to everlasting life and the beatific vision.

And what is the happiness of heaven? Words cannot describe, but barely hint at, the inexpressible jubilation of heaven. The Bible gives us a glimpse. Heaven is the ultimate destination and permanent abode of the faithful. Death, mourning, pain, and suffering will be no more. Peace and felicity will be everlasting. Death is not a stygian terminus but a passageway to heaven. The angels and our deceased loved ones will greet us with carols of celebration in heaven. We see mere reflections of God here on earth; we will see God face-to-face in heaven.

Bible verses bear out the existence of hell as an inferno of everlasting and unquenchable fire. Whether one should take the verses in a literal or figurative vein is a moot point. This much is not debatable. Hell is the permanent severance and separation of God and obdurate evildoers. A person damned to hell will never know a trace of happiness for all eternity. A person who spends his life rejecting God will be rejected by God upon death. A just God could not act otherwise. God vouchsafes mercy and forgiveness to every sinner throughout his life. Death closes the door to forgiveness forevermore. Even if God were to open the door, the impious man would slam it shut, himself. There is no love in him, he would never desire to share the company of a God who is love.

I reiterate that our purpose for being created is to know, love, and serve God and fellow man. Concretely, we do so by keeping the ten commandments. God reveals Himself through the perfect design and harmony of the universe, through the sacred scriptures, and through our expressions of love for each other. We gain insight into the wisdom, justice, goodness and love of God through communion with nature, study of the sacred scriptures, and loving relationships we have with others. God reveals Himself in a personal way through the daily events of our life.

We express our love for God by living up to the canons of our religion, especially through public worship and private devotions.

Holy scripture instructs and warns that we must serve God with joy and gratitude for our abundance of every kind. Otherwise, we will serve in hunger and thirst, in nakedness and utter poverty, the enemies God will send against us. We express our love for others by performing spiritual and corporal works of mercy. We who are well-fed must feed the hungry.

We who are virtuous must go all lengths to convert the sinner. God calls upon us to serve Him on an individual level. Although we share the same human nature, no two individuals are exactly alike. God has endowed each of us with unique talents, abilities, and strengths. Therefore, it follows that God will commit some special work or mission to each of us. We cannot understand fully God's master plan in this life. But God does nothing for naught. Whatever happens to us, happens for a definite reason. God makes no mistakes. All life's experiences can be directed to serve and give glory to God. We can serve God through acceptance of the hardship, adversity, sickness, and suffering God calls upon us to endure. Disappointment, uncertainty, even periods of spiritual desolation will be in store for us. Trust in God. He will guide us through every trial and tribulation if we are faithful. God will reward our forbearance with the kingdom of heaven.

CHAPTER TEN

Catholicism Today

In 1995 the Catholic population topped one billion people worldwide (about one out of every six people is Catholic). In the same year, in the U.S. there were 60 million Catholics, comprising the largest religion in the country (about one out of every four people is Catholic). These figures represent an impressive rate of growth of the laity; however, it is another matter for priests, secular or religious, as well as sisters and brothers. Despite an increase of vocations in Africa and Asia, the global statistics are bleak, especially in Europe, North, and South America. As of 1990, the number of priests in the world fell from about 420,000 to 403,000 with no reversal of decline. In the U.S., from the apex year of 1967 when there were about 60,000 priests, there are now approximately 50,000. In 1967 there were about 182,000 nuns while today there are about 94,000 in the U.S., an even more drastic drop. Moreover, deaths and resignations of priests now exceed ordinations, while the average age of priests, sisters and brothers (there are only about 6,500 brothers in the U.S.) continues to climb. The future does not bode well. In 1967 there were over 42,500 students enrolled in Catholic seminaries; there are now about 6,500, a precipitous drop of 85%.

Why this crisis in vocations while the Catholic laity burgeons? Critics of the Second Vatican Council are quick to point out the steep decline began right after the conclusion of Vatican II. They decry the relaxation of strictures for diocesan priests and religious orders, the end of the Tridentine Mass (Latin mass), and the modernization of ancient church practices. The dedractors claim the lines of distinction between the clergy, religious, and laity have blurred so there is no inducement for young people to consider a vocation. Proponents of the Second Vatican Council argue that the dramatic changes in church liturgy and praxis were vital to keep the church abreast of the modern world. They applaud the augmented involvement of the laity in ecclesiastical affairs (especially in participation in the mass) and attribute the explosive growth of laity to these developments. Rightfully, the supporters of Vatican II assert that sanctity does not depend on one's station in life. The same degree of holiness is possible in marriage as the ordained life. We are all equal members of the Body of Christ, equally loved by God.

Personally, I think both factions have valid points. There is no question that there exists a dearth of vocations. I submit that our modern way of life does not encourage them. Materialism, hedonism, and ego-worship are conditions sanctioned by today's society. Parents of today's small families (in Italy the birth rate is down to 1.3 child per family) do not encourage their children to enter religious life. Affluence and creature comforts are sought after by masses of people. Personal freedom and individualism are extolled. Priests, sisters and brothers eschew the "good life" championed by a secularized society; they must forgo wealth, sex, and some measure of personal freedom as they must follow the direction of their superiors. In addition, many Catholics today are not in accord with official church teachings. A great majority of Catholics disagree with Church teaching on pre-marital sex and family planning. Many advocate contraception and even abortion. A considerable number of Catholics are divorced, do not attend weekly mass nor believe in the real presence of Christ in the Eucharist; some deny the divinity of Christ. The reality of a nuclear family, father, mother, and children, has been attenuated shockingly. The number of single parent families has increased from 3.8 million in 1970 to 10.1 million in 1991. In 1970 almost 400,000 babies were born to single mothers while in 1989 more than 1,000,000 babies were born out of wedlock. This trend is global with unwed motherhood on the rise everywhere, reaching a third of all births in Europe. With the liberation of women in industrialized countries, with the concommitant upswing in feminism, the traditional concept of the nuclear family has been sabotaged. Women working with expanded earning power makes it easier to end unhappy marriages. But the children of divorced parents suffer from the lack of a mother or father. There is precious little time for a working parent to devote to the children unassisted. And the poverty level of children of single parent households is much greater than that of stable, intact families.

Certainly, such a social milieu cannot nurture a climate for growth of vocations. Yes, the power of Satan is immense in this age of non-reason, this century when he has been let loose upon it *"Woe to the earth and to the sea, for the devil hath come down upon it with great wrath, knowing that his time is short."* (Revelation 12:12) And, yet, we must not overlook the manifold positive developments taking place. A recent survey by Father Andrew Greeley, "Religion Around the World", indicates that belief in

God and religious practice are making a rebound. The report concludes that God is not dead in the lives of people. More evidence of this turnaround took place in Paris in 1994 when 100,000 people from thirty nations came for a five-day Christian gathering. Brother Roger, a Protestant theologian from the Taize community, convened believers who were Protestants, Catholics, and Orthodox. Who can forget the 500,000 people, mostly youngsters, who convened in Denver, Colorado in 1993 to celebrate mass with the Pope? And what of the 4 million people who poured into Manila, Philippines early in 1995 from all over the world, again, to celebrate mass with the Pope.

John Cardinal O'Connor composed a forceful pastoral letter to the N.Y. archdiocese in 1992 in which he detailed unfolding milestones in the growth of the church. The mass and sacraments are now celebrated in the local languages, although Tridentine (Latin) masses are available. The divine office is now prayed by laypersons since its adaptation into the vernacular. The Marriage Tribunal is being utilized to restore peace of mind to many Catholics who want to judge the validity of their marriage. Lay participation has proliferated with laypersons now holding key positions in diocesan offices, parishes, and schools. Priests now have more time to celebrate mass and administer the sacraments. The Rite of Christian Initiation of Adults program is an innovation that has guided converts into the church as well as furnishing present Catholics a fuller understanding of their faith. Ecumenism has made great strides in recent years. The Pope has extended the olive palm to all religions through open dialogue. The Vicar of Christ has called for Christian unity and mutual respect and understanding of non-Christian faiths. In his encyclical *Ut Unum Sint* (That Thy May Be One) proclaimed in 1995,

Pope John Paul II pleads for everyone to work for full and visible communion, especially Catholic bishops. This commitment is bringing to fruition the desire for unity of Our Lord: *"I pray that they may all be one. Father! May they be in us, just as you are in me and I am in you."* (John 17:21)

The fruit of this effort has been a magnified spirit of cooperation and reconciliation between Catholicism and other religions. In fact, many Protestant church leaders and Orthodox patriarchs have renewed their vow of unity efforts. Another exciting innovation is the restoration of the permanent diaconate. This apostolate allows married and single men to help priests by administering some of the sacraments and doing work in the parish, hospital, and prisons. The number of permanent deacons in the U.S. has grown consistently over the years and numbered over 11,000 in 1994, up 3,400 since 1984. Finally, the pastoral letter reflects on the ever increasing number of Catholics engaged in works of justice called the "Social Gospel" including the corporal works of mercy and campaigns against racism, religious bigotry, abortion, and the despoiling of our environment.

Other critical sectors in which the church strives and thrives are in education, hospitals, hospices for the dying, counseling for troubled youth and pregnant teenagers, and treatment centers for drug addicts. The Catholic Church in the U.S. has a network of 20,000 parishes, almost 9,000 elementary and secondary schools, more than 200 colleges and universities, and more than 550 hospitals. This social service system is open to all people, encompassing all races, creeds, and economic classes. The American Catholic school system is the world's largest, private education system, with more than 4,000,000 students and 160,000 lay and religious teachers. For over 1,600 years the Catholic Church has run schools to educate and preserve the culture. Most of this time the work was carried on by religious orders. What a proud and noble tradition! In the U.S. over 8,000,000 Catholic children are receiving religious instruction (Confraternity of Christian Doctrine) in Catholic and public schools. They are being taught Catholic doctrine and the message of community service. Superlative values are being inculcated, such as non-violence, brotherhood, compassion, honesty, industry, and loyalty to God, country, and church. Please, God, that we always support our church's social and educational programs.

CHAPTER ELEVEN

Ways To Improve The Social Climate and World Outlook

There has been a sea change in our society since world War II. The G.I. Bill afforded the opportunity for many people to go to college who were previously unable to do so. Postwar economic boom brought prosperity and affluence to the middle class. Most Catholic immigrants and their children assimilated into the middle class. The Golden Age continued through the 50's and 60's. Those were hopeful days for our ethnic minorities with the advent of peace and civil rights marches and legislation. Vatican II was the springboard for the aforementioned benign developments in our church. Many persons, including Catholic priests, sisters, and brothers were dedicated to worthy causes and ideals.

However, some of the serious social ills confronting that era remain unresolved and, perhaps, are getting worse, namely; poverty, crime, drug abuse, corruption in government and private spheres, social injustice and racism, divorce and broken homes, sexual promiscuity among adults and adolescents, ecological depredation, and so forth. Making matters worse today is the plague of AIDS. These are grave problems that grip our entire world. These are complex issues that are agonizing to deal with and without a panacea. But we cannot sit back and watch in idle helplessness. I am convinced that if we all work hard to make a better world, we can make it happen. It will take the collaboration of people of all races, religions, and socio-economic backgrounds working together in good faith. Greed, selfishness, prejudice and immorality must first be overcome on a personal level before we can make the dream of a better world come true. I also believe we cannot rely only on ourselves or others to get the job done. We must turn back to God and keep His commandments. I firmly believe we must uphold traditional religious teachings and spirituality, whatever one's faith, to counteract the evils that abound in the world.

On the brighter side, there is a myriad of auspicious advancements taking place throughout the world. Thank God for the incipience of global demilitarization, the end of the cold war, the collapse of Communism, and the emergence of freedom and democracy for people around the world. A greater number of people are living in freedom than ever before. According to a report published by Freedom House, almost 70% of the world's population now enjoy partial or full freedom. Many nations now free were captive to Communism. Within the past few years, billions of people have tasted freedom with the institution of democratic governments. The natural rights philosophers, Thomas Hobbs and John Locke, believed that a government should protect the inalienable rights of life, liberty, and prosperity of its denizens. The people of a nation should have a "social contract" with the government which insures that the government will rule with the consent of the governed. The growth of democracy throughout the world has created never-before educational and economic opportunities for poor people. As a result they have acquired pecuniary and political power.

There have been vast improvements in technology, communication, scientific advances, health and sanitation systems, and methods of growing food. The peace dividend from a reduction of world armaments and military spending can be a boon to all mankind. We have the means to transform our planet if we beat our swords into plowshares. We have the means to eradicate global poverty, hunger, disease, and illiteracy if we are willing to distribute our wealth and resources equitably. Through governmental initiative such as massive new aid to anti-poverty programs, to primary and secondary education, to academic and vocational training for school dropouts and welfare recipients, we can close the widening gap between the haves and have-nots.

We have the means and minds to accomplish these goals. Now it's a matter of heart, a need for great love. All things are possible if we love God and our neighbor. You might well ask, "Who is my neighbor?" My unswerving answer is every single person in our global village. World peace is still a vision to be realized, but we are getting closer. Pray for world peace every day. Catholics pray the rosary as requested by Mary, the mother of Jesus. Our Blessed Mother is keeping her promises, we are witnessing the conversion of Russia before our very eyes. We are going to die; ergo, we should advert to the last four things: death, judgment, heaven or hell. In Matthew, Chapter 25, our Lord, Jesus, tells us we will be judged on our spiritual and corporal works of mercy...feeding the hungry, clothing the naked, sheltering the homeless, and such. We are not going to be judged on how much money, property or prestige we have. To quote from our living saint, Mother

Teresa of India, "Each one has a mission to fulfill, a vision of love. At the hour of death when we come face-to-face with God, we are going to be judged on love, not how much we have done, but how much love we put into our actions."

In 1995 Cardinal O'Connor addressed the national meeting of the Institute of Religious Life consisting of priests, sisters and brothers. In his keynote speech, he implored his audience to "embrace the cross." He told them, "If vocations are lacking one must ask how visible is the joy in which we carry it...The way of the cross is the only thing that works." Another speaker, Father Benedict Groeschel, C.F.R., director of the Office of Spiritual Development of the Archdiocese of New York declaimed, "The religious communities that will thrive in the future will be smaller and will require more maturity on the part of a member, a firm commitment to the faith and an observance of communal and individual poverty." Let us recall the life and works of Saint Vianney. He reviled the false values of the world. Instead, he preached and practiced penance, fasting, humility, poverty, an intense prayer life, and performance of works of mercy. He lived on the cross. In fact, he said it was a sweet thing to die when one has lived on the cross. Our Blessed Mother, in apparitions springing forth throughout the world, urgently pleads the same message. Will the world repent while there is time?

God loves all His children, Protestant, Catholic, Jewish, Moslem, Buddhist, Hindu, and makes it possible for all to enter his kingdom. To its everlasting credit, the Catholic Church upheld, at the Second Vatican Council, that salvation is possible not only for non-Catholics but for non-Christians. "In ways known only to Himself, God can lead those who, through no fault of their own, are ignorant of the Gospel to that faith in God without which it is impossible to please Him." (Dogmatic Constitution on the Church, Luman Gentium, 14).

The key is not believing the right doctrine or acknowledging God in a prescribed form, the Good Thief on the cross did neither of these, but in obeying God's simple decree, which subsumes all the dogmas of every religion: to love Him and each other. Doing this displays faith, faith that there is a God who rewards good and punishes evil, that God, Himself, is good, that His way of love is the only way to happiness and peace, both on earth and in heaven.

Love Him and each other. The rest is commentary. If people must have doctrines and rituals, so be it. But they should not be divisive or against brotherhood. God does not choose and save a few people, whatever they call themselves, by showing them the light and giving them the only true set of beliefs. No, God chooses and saves all people who know, love, and serve Him. Salvation has come through Jesus Christ for all peoples. Whether or not all peoples come to know and accept this central tenet of Christianity, the fact remains. This is not to say that all persons are guaranteed salvation. An unrepentant life spent doing evil deserves separation from God, in fact, is to choose separation from God. The wages of sin are death and hell.

Even belief in God, without righteous living and good works, is not sufficient to be a guarantee of individual salvation. Faith without works is dead. I relish the conviction that all persons of good will, that is, all who seek God and live upright lives according to the inner light of conscience, receive salvation through Jesus Christ, even though they may not acknowledge Him in this life. I am convinced that these souls come to know and love Jesus in heaven. Having spent their lives loving others and seeking God's highest truth, they will feel right at home with Him.

Sincere persons follow the dictates of their conscience and embrace religious truth as God reveals it to them. It may not be the way He has revealed Himself to me, but any good that is done, any knowledge that is attained, is a gift from an all-loving God. God reveals Himself in different ways to all people. Remember that God is bigger than all of us put together. We cannot exhaust all there is to know about God. We are human, and are limited by the way we look at things. The more we understand what others think about God, the more we can understand God. We can learn from everyone, and we have God's pledge: *"When you look for me, you will find me. Yes, when you seek me with all your heart, you will find me with you."* (Jeremiah 29:13-24)

Truth is universal, and all people of every faith can share in the fullness of truth. Truth in spiritual matters, that is, our relationship with God, is how he reveals himself to the earnest seeker. God has a plan of salvation tailor-made for every individual. The good Lord will show you the way, the set of beliefs, the manner of worship He wants you to follow when you love Him. He is infinite love in infinite variety. This is why I believe He made so many of us - each of us reflects, *sui generis*, a part of God's infinite variety. That is His way. And how can you be sure you are walking with God on the path He has laid out for you? By the fruit you produce. *"You will know them by their deeds! Do you ever pick grapes from thornbushes or figs from prickly plants? Never! Any sound tree bears good fruit, while a decayed tree bears bad fruit. A sound tree cannot bear bad fruit any more than a decayed tree can bear good fruit."* (Matthew 7:16-18) It follows that a loving nature produces acts of love.

Prayer is communication with God. Prayer is not stilted verbiage repeated by rote. It is not a litany of sanctimonious cant,reserved for paying homage to God. It is not lip service. Prayer is the conformity of our lives with the will of God. Prayer should be a consciousness of God in our lives. No one is so busy frittering away his life on details that he cannot find a few moments each day to think about God. An ephemeral reflection on God's goodness or an utterance of thanksgiving for His many blessings does not take up much time, but means so much to our loving Father. Morning and evening prayers as well as grace offered at meals, need not be wordy. Of course, there are times when we should devote all our thoughts to God at length. When we attend services at church and synagogue we must put our quotidian concerns aside. We can recite the liturgy or formal orisons and use the time to meditate on God and our lives.

Why do we pray? We pray to adore God, to offer thanks for our blessings, to ask forgiveness for our sins, and to petition help. God always listens to and answers our prayers. Sometimes God says no to our petitions as He knows what is best for us, not necessarily what we desire. For our part, we must make a trustful surrender to divine providence. God manifests His will in subtle ways. If we are strong of faith, we will grasp God's message and accept His will. For whom do we pray? We should pray for the living and the dead. We pray for ourselves, family, friends, and enemies. We supplicate God's mercy and help for the poor, sick, oppressed, troubled, for all who are suffering. Our prayers must be sincere and humble. Keep in mind that we are raising our hearts to God, not trying to impress others with our holiness. We must pray with patient perseverance and not be dismayed if God does not answer our prayers immediately. Contemplation or meditation is prayer not dependent upon the use of spoken words. Through contemplation we may attain a mystical awareness of God's being. There are structured paths to meditation: through the intellect, the emotions, sensory awareness and breath control, and various skilled disciplines, including singing, chanting, dancing, and yoga.

Two helpful guidebooks for interested persons are *Seeds of Contemplation* by Thomas Merton and *How to Meditate* by Lawrence Le Shan. A constant companion of Saint Vianney was the spiritual guide, *The Knowledge and Love of Our Lord Jesus Christ*, by Father Jean Baptiste Saint-Jure. This treatise covers God's control of all events and the practice of conformity to the will of God. There are three plateaus of the spiritual life: The purgative stage in which we subdue the passions; the illuminative stage in which we draw close to God through good works and contemplation; and the highest stage, the unitive state in which we are bound to God through mystical experience.

Mysticism is the direct apprehension of, and communion with, God. Saint Vianney was graced with ecstatic or mystical union with God, especially during adoration of the Blessed Sacrament. A mystical experience is beyond the scope of sense perception and human reasoning; the presence and power of God is initiated by a person with or without benefit of contemplation. Mystical experiences are rare but we all undergo them in our lifetime. A true mystical experience is unmistakably recognized as such by the subject. His whole being is transfused with God consciousness. Although the subject is incapable of expressing his rapture in words, he becomes certain of the presence of God in the world. The experience usually lasts only a few moments, and the subject is in a passive state, completely relaxed and motionless. In this experience the subject's ego is swept into and merged with the expanding universe. He sees each person and object as part of a greater whole and becomes oblivious of space and time. His sense of far and near, past, present, and future are suspended in the unitive state. There is a realm of experience that is beyond space and time which is realized in the unitive state. The mystical experience transcends the realm of the senses and the intellect. It provides insight into the real nature of eternal objects, man, and God. Man's soul attains union with nature, fellow man, and God through the mystical experience. Unlike prayer and contemplation, which are initiated by a person, the mystical experience is endued by God without human initiative.

Pierre Teilhard de Chardin (1881-1950) was a Catholic priest, theologian, and scientist of the first magnitude. Chardin formulated a cosmology in which religion and science were not merely recognized but vibrantly synthesized. In this evolutionary conception of the universe as a whole, everything is harmoniously integrated and exalted. All forms of matter chemical, plant, animal, are being gradually spiritualized through love. In the grand scheme of things, love is the unfaltering engine that drives all creation. Chardin was a staunch proponent of the theory of evolution; he affirmed that man's physiological evolution was complete but that man's spiritual evolution would continue until the global Zeitgeist, the spirit of the age, will be love. The Incarnation of God bestowed upon us the insuperable generosity of His love and ushered in the Messianic Age. The nativity of Jesus Christ was a watershed in man's spiritual development. The propulsive Christogenesis is only in its embryonic stage, a scant two thousand years old. Man is now only dimly aware that his mission and redemption rest in growing in the love of God. When man's love of God blazes into a conflagration consuming the world, transforming the material into the spiritual, then Jesus will appear on earth in glory. The consummation of the world is to be realized in the ubiquitous consciousness of Christ. In the fullness of time, the world will be perfected in all pervading love.

Chardin vigorously resisted Manichean duality, that is, the belief in the absolute and independent existence of two diametrically opposed principles or forces in the world good and evil. Then how do we reckon with all the evil that abounds in man and in the world? Evil is the negation and privation of love. Satan is a conscious, extremely intelligent, angelic being. In essence, he was created by God to be good and loving. Through free will, Satan repudiated his Creator, who is Love, and chose to be irreformably diabolic. Of crucial import is that Satan is a created, dependent being. Satan is nowise on a par with God. God is omnipotent; Satan is not. Satan's power, the power of evil, is infinitely inferior to God's power, the power of love. Satan roams the earth and torments us for a time. When love reigns in all hearts, Satan will be vanquished. Evil will cease to exist in our lives.

The idea of evolution and progress is basic to the thinking of Teilhard de Chardin. He declared roundly that scientific progress will lead to an active awareness of God. Technological strides will enable man to clearly apprehend his progress as a working out of a divine plan. Order and design presuppose intelligence. The order and design evident everywhere in the universe presuppose a supreme intelligence. The effect of Chardin's writings is to present a schema of the spiritual evolution of man and all creation. God is the breath and pulse of life and the force that moves the planets in perfect harmony. God is the source of the achievements of science. Man strives to conquer space, which separates him from other men. Time, also, imposes separation on people. Chardin enunciated that space and time are spiritual in substance and merged them in the realm of the spirit. Man can conquer the vastness of space through his visionary power. His mind can span all time. His heart can spiritualize matter. Man is a true son of God as he responds to a divine call within himself to seek the Father with his mind and heart.

CHAPTER TWELVE

Author's Reflections

In learning to live in God's love I have encountered loving people of many faiths, and I have a profound respect for them all. And, while I have learned of God from holy persons of many religions, so much of my personal inspiration has been from my own Catholic Church that I would like to share some further reflections.

The Catholic Church has flourished since its inception despite serious setbacks and temporary declines due to heresies, schisms, and the Protestant Reformation. Today there are over 1 billion Catholics, making the Catholic Church the largest religion in the world. Membership is increasing steadily, with no signs of abatement. I attribute this phenomenal growth to absorption, adaptation, and assimilation. Catholicism has drawn upon and soaked up the mores, cultures and religious beliefs and practices of people around the world for the last two millennia. It has avoided extremism in its relentless drive for the happy medium, the balance between conservatism and liberalism. This is not to say that the Catholic Church has compromised the Gospel; rather, the church has recognized that such things as culture and customs do not necessarily pose a conflict with God's moral law, and therefore an array of people of many backgrounds have found a home in the Catholic Church.

Catholics who want to sing, jump for joy and praise the Lord like Pentecostals, no problem, they can attend charismatic services. Catholics who want to become totally immersed in the written Word of God and be involved in evangelization can find a niche in the charismatic renewal, too. Catholics, who prefer traditional acts of worship, even Latin Mass, there's a place for them, individually or within a group such as *Opus Dei*. Catholics who want to be active in social and economic change may prefer the liberation movement. There is a home for almost anyone within the Catholic Church. This may be what gives Catholicism its staying power. The indisputable wisdom of the Catholic Church is that it offers something for almost everyone. The one type of individual for which there is little room in the Catholic Church is the extremist. The Islamic fundamentalists, the Moral Majority, the Rabbi Kahane Jews those who set themselves apart as Sons of Light opposed to the Sons of Darkness (which category includes everyone not of themselves) cannot abide the eclecticism and universalism of the Catholic Church. The very nature of these groups, exclusivist is the antithesis of the Catholic (which means "universal") Church. A compulsion to be the sole light-bearer generally leads to separation (this has an ancient precedent). A recent example is found in the schism of French Archbishop Lefebre's Society of St. Pius X.

On the other hand, a luminary such as Mother Teresa of India is recognized by people of good will the world over as an example of the love of God made manifest, and an example of the best of the Catholic Church. Her philosophy is worth pondering. "Never let anything so fill you with sorrow as to make you forget the joy of the Risen Christ." Furthermore, we should be able to see Jesus Christ (sometimes in a distressing disguise) in all people, including society's outcasts;that is the homeless, convicts, drug addicts et al.

Dear fellow pilgrims, these are a few final thoughts I would like to share with you. Holiness is not reserved for spiritual giants like Saint John Vianney but for everyone. Too many people are complacent about their moral and spiritual lives. Their attitude is that they're not so bad and that God will forgive their sins anyway. This attitude leads to backsliding and spiritual sluggishness. It produces a lax conscience and a presumptuous posture, that is, that faith alone, regardless of moral conduct, is sufficient for salvation. Saint Vianney struggled his entire life for spiritual perfection; this is an ideal we should all strive for despite our sinful habits. God wants us to be blameless in His sight. Whatever God's plans for us, we must ever keep in mind that God expects us to become holy. Saint Vianney believed that we have a foretaste of heaven, purgatory, and hell in this life. Heaven is for souls closely united with God while alive; purgatory is reserved for those who are not dead to themselves and the world; hell is the destination of the impious.

God's thoughts are not our thoughts and His ways are not our ways. We may not know God's plans for us at all times but we will always know His will - that we love Him, neighbor, and self; that we grow spiritually through our faith in God and through good works; that we turn our lives to God and away from sin. The most important elements in doing God's will are acceptance and trust. If we have faith and trust in God, we believe He has a plan for us that is always in our best interest. We may not understand why things happen the way they do, but we should never lose confidence in God's love and concern for us. Saint Vianney was prepared to give up his quest for the priesthood when he was expelled from the seminary; he did not become bitter and resentful towards God.

Christians must never allow hardships and sufferings to overshadow the joy of the resurrected Christ. Sometimes a tragedy or bad experience can lead us to God. Self-discipline and perseverance are vital to successful living. We must commend our lives to God each and every day. God loves us even though we sin, even when we don't love Him. Never despair, no matter how often we fall into sin, ask forgiveness and repent. Salvation starts today! Don't tarry in turning your life over to God, for there may be no tomorrow. When a person entrusts his life to God, there is a gradual change of character. God gives the grace to overcome sin and wrongdoing and to live righteously. The crosses we bear will become a source of great peace and happiness in time. Saint Vianney's life was full of penances, fasts, self-mortification, and battles with the devil, yet he often avowed that the greatest cross was to have no cross.

In my role as a teacher I have sought to instill sound values in my students. In turn my students have taught me a most valuable lesson, that the essence of these values and my work is love. My advice to you, dear reader, is not to dwell on how much money or possessions you have accumulated, nor even your worthy personal accomplishments, but rather on the love you put into all your actions. Don't miss a single opportunity to share your time and talents to help the needy. If possible, become involved in some charitable or social work on a voluntary basis. Trillions of dollars and natural resources are being squandered by world governments on the military and by us, the citizens, on consumerism while people go hungry and homeless. This is a great evil we must fight. And don't dare tell yourself it's not humanly possible, or that *"You have the poor with you always."* (Mark 14:7) Jesus said these dismal words because he read our hearts true. With God all things are possible.

I would like to conclude this book by echoing the challenge issued by Saint John Vianney to the parishioners and pilgrims of his time. Many of these people were just as materialistic, immoral, and godless as many people today. Yet they listened, took his message to heart, and were converted. It is my confidence that such a religious revival is possible today if we embrace Saint John Vianney's exhortations.

Reflect on your actions this day. Have they evinced a full measure of love? Make up your mind right now that you will make some sacrifice, perform some spiritual or corporal work of mercy for someone in need each day. I believe that we are all instruments of God's will and are meant to help each other on life's journey. Truly, we do not know the day we will be summoned before God for judgment. Be prepared to render an exemplary account. I beg you to take these words to heart. Saint John Vianney, pray for us who have recourse to thee!

Bibliography

The Cure' D'Ars: St. Jean-Marie Baptiste Vianney
    By Abbe' Francis Trochu
    Tan Books and Publishers, Inc.
    Rockford, Illinois

The Cure' of Ars

    By Father Bartholomew O'Brien
    Tan Books and Publishers, Inc.
    Rockford, Illinois

The Little Catechism of the Cure' D'Ars

    (formerly titled The Cure' of Ars to His People)
    Tan Books and Publishers, Inc.
    Rockford, Illinois

The Cure' D'Ars Today

    By George William Rutler
    Ignatius Press
    San Francisco, California

The Catholic Church at The End of An Age

    By Ralph Martin
    Ignatius Press
    San Francisco, California

A Spiritual Guide to Eternal Life

    By Alexander LaPerchia
    Philosophical Library
    New York City, New York

A New York City Teacher Learns Love

    By Alexander LaPerchia
    Magnificat Press
    Avon, New Jersey

Appendix

RETREAT AT ARS FOR PRIESTS
DEACONS, AND SEMINARIANS

October 6, 1986

Pope John Paul II

THE FIRST MEDITATION

1. *"As the Father sent me, I too send you...Receive
the Holy Spirit"* *(Jn 20:21-22).*

Dear brothers, it is Christ who chooses us; he
sends us as he was sent by the Father, and he imparts
the Holy Spirit to us. Our priesthood is rooted in the
missions of the Divine Person, in their mutual gift in
the heart of the Holy Trinity. *"The grace of the Holy
Spirit...comes to be transmitted by episcopal ordination. Then, through the sacrament of orders, the
bishops make the sacred ministers sharers in this
spiritual gift"* (see Encyclical *Dominum et
Vivificantem, no. 25).* Priests and deacons too share
in this grace.

Our mission is a mission of salvation. *"God sent
his Son into the world, so that the world might be
saved through him"* (Jn 3:17). Jesus preached the
Good News of the Kingdom; he chose and formed
his apostles; he accomplished the work of redemption by he Cross and the Resurrection. Following
the apostles, we are associated in a particular manner
with his work of salvation, to make it present and
effective everywhere in the world. Saint Jean Marie
Vianney went so far as to say, "Without the priest,

the death and passion of our Lord would be of no use. It is the priest who continues the work of Redemption on earth" (*Jean-Marie Vianney, Cure d'Ars, sa pensee, son coeur,* presented by Fr. Bernard Nodet, Le Puy, 1958, p.100; hereafter cited as Nodet).

It is this that we must put into effect: it is, accordingly, not our work, but the design of the Father and salvific work of the Son. The Holy Spirit makes use of our mind, of our mouth, of our hands. It is our especial task to proclaim the Word unceasingly, in order to spread the gospel, and to translate it in such a way that we touch people's hearts without altering it or diminishing it; and it is ours to perform once again the act of offering that Jesus made at the Last Supper and his acts of pardon for sinners.

2. It is not only a commission that we have received, a significant function to carry out in the service of the people of God. People can speak of priesthood as of a profession or function, including the function of presiding over the eucharistic assembly. But we are not reduced by this to functionaries.

This is so first of all because we are marked in our very souls through ordination with a special character that configures us to Christ the Priest, so that we are made capable of acting personally in the name of Christ the Head (cf. decree *Presbyterorum Ordinis,* no. 2). Certainly, it is true that we are taken from among men and that we remain close to them, Christians with them", as Saint Augustine said. But we are "set apart", totally consecrated to the work of salvation (cf. ibid., no.3): "the function of the priest, in that it is united to the episcopal order, shares in the authority with which Christ himself builds up, sanctifies and governs his Body" (ibid., no.2). It is the Second Vatican Council that recalls this to us.

We are at one and the same time in the Christian assembly and in front of it, to signify that the initiative comes from God, from the Head of the Body, and that the Church receives it. Sent in the name of Christ, we have been sanctified by him with a particular qualification; this remains, and profoundly touches our existence as baptized persons. The Cure d'Ars had extremely direct formulations to speak of this: "It is the priest whom God puts on earth as another mediator between the Lord and the poor sinner" (Nodet, p.99): we should say today that he participates in a specific way in the mission of the sole Mediator, Jesus Christ.

This implies a consequence in our life each day. It is normal that we seek continually to conform ourselves to Christ, whose ministers we are, not only in our ministerial acts but also in our thoughts, the attachment of our heart, and our conduct, as disciples who go to the extent of reproducing the mysteries of his life, as Father Chevrier says. Obviously, this presupposes a genuine intimacy with Christ, in prayer. All our person and all our life refer to Christ. *Imitamini quod tractatis.* All the baptized are called to holiness, but our consecration and our mission make it a particular duty for us to aim at holiness, whether we are diocesan or religious priests, by means of the riches inherent in our priesthood and the requirements of our ministry within the people of God.

It is true that the sacraments derive their efficacy from Christ, not from our dignity. We are his poor and humble instruments, who must not attribute to ourselves the merit of the grace that is transmitted; but we are responsible instruments and, by the holiness of the minister, souls are better disposed to cooperate with grace.

In the Cure d'Ars we see precisely a priest who

was not satisfied with an external accomplishment of the acts of redemption; he shares in this in his very being, in his love of Christ, in his constant prayer, in the offering of his trials or his voluntary mortifications. As I said already to the priests at Notre Dame in Paris, on May 30, 1980, "The Cure d'Ars remains for all countries an unequaled model both of the carrying out of the ministry and of the holiness of the minister."

3. In other words, dear friends, we may well admire the splendor of the ministerial priesthood, and likewise the vocation to the religious life, because there is a certain relationship between the two. You know the saying of the Cure d'Ars: "Oh, the priest is something great! If he knew it, he would die" (Nodet, p.99). Indeed, what a wonderful thing it is to exercise our threefold priestly ministry as bishops or priests, a ministry that is indispensable to the Church:

The ministry of the one who proclaims the Good News: to make Jesus Christ known; to put men into a true relationship to him; to watch over the authenticity and fidelity of the Faith, so that it may neither be lacking nor changed nor sclerotic; and also to keep alive in the Church the impulse of evangelization, and to form apostolic workers.

The ministry of the one who dispenses the mysteries of God: to make them present in an authentic manner, especially to make present the paschal mystery by means of the Eucharist and of forgiveness of sins; to permit the baptized to have access to these, and to prepare them for this. The laity will never be able to be delegated to such ministries; a priestly ordination, which permits one to act in the name of Christ the Head, is necessary.

The ministry, finally, of the pastor: to build up

and maintain the Communion among Christians, in the community that is entrusted to us, with the other diocesan communities, all linked to the successor of Peter. Before any specialization in view of his personal competences, and in accord with his bishop, the priest is in fact the minister of Communion: in a Christian community that often risks rupture or closing in on itself, he ensures both the gathering together of the family of God and its openness. His priesthood confers on him the power to lead the priestly people (cf. Letter of Holy Thursday 1979, no.5).

4. Thus the specific identity of the priest appears clearly. In any case, after the debates of the last twenty years, this is now less and less a matter of discussion. Yet the very small number of priests and of priestly ordinations in many countries could lead certain faithful, or even priests to be resigned to this shortage, on the pretext that the role of the laity had been better rediscovered and put into practice.

It is true that the council had the happy intuition of locating the ministerial priesthood again in the perspective of the apostolic mission within all the people of God. It prevented priests from making their priesthood an independent possession, detached from this people. It emphasized the fundamental task of proclaiming the Word, which prepares the ground for faith, and thus for the sacraments. It gave a better expression to the relationship between the priesthood of the priest and that of the bishop, and showed its relationship to the ordained ministry of the deacons and to the common priesthood of all the baptized, thanks to which all can and must have access to the riches of grace (adoption as sons, life of Christ, the Holy Spirit, the sacraments), and make their life a spiritual offering, bear witness to Christ in the world as disciples, and take their part in the apostolate and the services of the Church.

However, precisely in order to exercise fully this prophetic, priestly, and royal role, the baptized need the ministerial priesthood. By means of it, in a privileged and tangible manner, the gift of the Divine Life received from Christ, the Head of the all the Body, is communicated to them. The more Christian the people become, the more they become aware of their dignity and of their active role in the Church, and the more they feel the need of priests who are truly priests. And this is true also in de-Christianized regions and in social milieus cut off from the Church (cf. discourse at Notre Dame, Paris, May 30, 1980, no.3). Laity and priests can never be resigned to see the number of priestly vocations and ordinations reduced, as is the case today in many dioceses. This resignation would be a bad sign for the vitality of the Christian people and would put its future and its mission at risk. It would be ambiguous to organize the Christian communities as if they could very largely do without the priestly ministry, under the pretext of facing the near future with realism. On the contrary, let us ask ourselves if we are doing all that is possible to awaken in the Christian people the awareness of the beauty and the necessity of the priesthood, to awaken vocations, to encourage them and bring them to maturity. I am happy to know that your vocations directors are taking new initiatives to issue the call again. Let us not weary in asking for prayers, so that the Lord of the harvest may send laborers.

Dear brothers, let us remain modest and humble, because this is a grace of the Lord, received for the service of others, and we are never truly worth of it. The Cure d'Ars said, "The priest does not exist for himself, he exists for you" (Nodet, p.102). But, like him, let us not cease to wonder at the greatness of our priesthood and to give thanks each moment.

And may you, dear seminarians, aspire even more to this sublime service of the Lord and of his Church, in joy and hope!

Prayer

Lord, like the Apostle Peter, we have all felt in our inmost lives the call to leave the tranquil banks and put out on the deep, to leave he nets of a human profession in order to be fishers of men;

You have called us through the Church, you have consecrated us and anointed us with your Spirit; you have sent us on ahead of you, to act in your name, at the service of all the members of the People of God, so that they may receive your message and your divine life more and more;

Make us constantly engaged in thanksgiving, and attentive to conform our whole life to the holiness of this ministry, you who live with the Father and the Holy Spirit for ever and ever.

THE SECOND MEDITATION

5. "I have made myself all things to all men, in order by all means to save some"
(I Cor 9:22).

The word *salvation* is one of those used most frequently by the Cure d'Ars. What does it mean for him? To be saved is to be delivered from the sin that separates from God, dries up the heart, and risks eternal separation from the love of God — which would be the worst unhappiness of all. To be saved is to live united to God, to see God. To be saved is likewise to be reintroduced into a true communion with others, because our sins very often consist in wounding the love of neighbor, justice, truth the respect for his goods and his body: all this is contrary to the will of God. There is a profound solidarity among all the members of the Body of Christ: one cannot love him without loving his brothers. Salvation therefore permits one to rediscover a filial relationship to God and a fraternal relationship to others.

The redemption of Christ has opened for all the possibility of salvation. The priest cooperates in redemption, preparing souls for it by preaching conversion and by giving pardon for sins. It was for their salvation that the Cure d'Ars wanted to be a priest: "To win souls for the Good God", as he said when he announced his vocation at the age of eighteen, as Saint Paul had said, "to win the greatest number" (I Cor 9:19). It was for this that Jean Marie Vianney spent himself to the point of exhaustion and undertook to do penance, as if to wrest from God the graces of conversion. He feared for their salvation and wept. And when he was tempted to run away from his heavy charge as parish priest, he came back, for the salvation of parishioners. We read in Saint Paul, "The love of Christ constrains us...now is the day of salvation" (2 Cor 5:14;6:2). "The priesthood", as Jean Marie Vianney also said, "is the love of the heart of Christ" (Nodet, p.100).

Dear brothers, many of our contemporaries seem to have become indifferent to the salvation of their souls. Are we sufficiently concerned about this loss of faith, or do we just resign ourselves?

Certainly, we have every reason to insist today on the love of God, who sent his Son to save and not to condemn. We have every reason to emphasize love rather than anxiety and fear. This is what the Cure d'Ars did, too.

Besides this, men are free to adhere or not to faith and salvation; they claim their freedom with loud voices, and the Church for her part wishes them to take the step of faith in freedom from external constraints (see *Dignitatis Humanac, no. 3)*, while safeguarding the moral obligation on each one to seek the truth and to hold onto it and to act in accordance with his conscience.

Finally, God himself is free with his gifts. Conversion is a grace. In the encyclical *Dominum et Vivificantem* (pt. 2, no. 47), I have shown that only the Holy Spirit permits us to become aware of the gravity of sin and of the tragedy of the loss of the sense of God, and gives the desire for conversion.

But our love for mankind cannot be resigned to seeing them deprive themselves of salvation. We cannot directly produce the conversion of souls, but we are responsible for the proclamation of the Faith, of the totality of the Faith and of its demands. We must invite our faithful to conversion and to holiness; we must speak the truth, warn, advise, and make them desire the sacraments that reestablish them in the grace of God. The Cure d'Ars considered this a formidable but necessary ministry: "If a pastor remains dumb when he sees God outraged and souls wandering away, woe to him!" We know with what care he prepared his Sunday homilies and his catechesis, and with what courage he recalled the requirements of the gospel, denounced sin, and invited men to make good the evil they had committed.

To convert, to heal, to save: three key words of our mission. The Cure d'Ars obviously stood truly in solidarity with his sinful people: he did everything to snatch souls from their sin and torpor and to lead them back to love: "Grant me the conversion of my parish, and I am ready to suffer whatever you wish for the rest of my life." It has been said that he had "a vision of salvation full of pathos": it may be that some expressions and a severe tone were inspired in him by Jansenism. Yet he was able to overcome this rigorism. He preferred to insist on the attractive side of virtue and on the mercy of God, for whom our sins are "like grains of sand". He showed the tenderness of the God who had been offended. His appeals followed the direct line of the appeals of the prophets (see Ezek 3:16, 21), of Jesus, of Saint Paul, and of Saint Augustine on the importance of salvation and the urgency of conversion. He feared that the priests might become apathetic and accustomed to the indifference of their faithful. How could we neglect his warning today?

6. *"Let yourselves be reconciled to God."*
This sentence of Saint Paul defines perfectly he ministry of Saint Jean Marie Vianney. He is known in all the world as the one who heard confession for ten to fifteen hours a day or even longer, and was still doing this up to five days before his death. Doubtless, we cannot transpose this literally into the rhythm of our priestly lives, but his attitude and his motivations challenge us vigorously.

The essential thing in his ministry of salvation was to offer forgiveness to repentant souls, at the price of an effort that does not cease to impress us. Do we accord the same importance to he sacrament of reconciliation? Are we ready to consecrate time to it?

Do we look hard enough in our cities and villages for the practical means to offer them the possibility of this sacrament? Do we try to renew the celebration of the sacrament, in conformity with the suggestions of the Church (confrontation with the gospel communal preparation made periodically, and so on), without ceasing to envisage the personal act of confession, at least for grave sins? In the last case, do we try to make people understand that this is a condition for participation in the Eucharist and also for the worthy celebration of the sacrament of marriage (see the *apostolic exhortation Reconciliatio et Paenitentia, no. 27*)? Do we appreciate the marvelous opportunity offered to us in this way to form consciences and to guide souls to a spiritual progress?

I know, dear friends, that many priests, with their bishop, have tried to take this practice up again, after a difficult period. I encourage you in this with all the force I possess. This was the object of the postsynodal document *Reconciliatio et Paenitentia.*

I know too that you encounter many difficulties: the shortage of priests, and above all the loss of affection on the part of the faithful for the sacrament of forgiveness. You say, "For a long time now, they no longer come to confession." That is indeed the problem! Does this not conceal a lack of faith, a lack of sense of sin, of the sense of the mediation of Christ and the Church, and low esteem for a practice known only in the deformations of routine?

Let us note what his vicar-general said to the Cure d'Ars: "There is not much love of God in this parish: you will put it there." The holy parish priest also found penitents without much fervor. However, because of his priestly attitude of holiness, a considerable crowd grasped the importance of the sacrament of forgiveness. What was the secret with which he attracted both believer and unbelievers, holy people and sinners? The Cure d'Ars, who was so hard in some sermons in order to castigate sin, was—like Jesus—very merciful in the encounter with each sinner. Father Monin said of him that he was a "fire of tenderness and mercy". He burned with the mercy of Christ.

We have here an extremely important aspect of evangelization. From the evening of Easter onward, the apostles were sent out to forgive sins. The gift of the Holy Spirit is bound to this power. And the Book of Acts continually comes back to the forgiveness of sins as the grace of the New Covenant (see Acts 2:38; 5:31; 10:43;13:38). This is the *leitmotiv* of the preaching of the apostles: "Let yourselves be reconciled."

These words are addressed to us, too, dear friends. Are we personally faithful in receiving forgiveness through the mediation of another priest?

7. It was to the Eucharist that Jean Marie Vianney wished to lead his penitent faithful. You know the central place that the Mass occupied in each of his days, and with what care he prepared himself for Mass and celebrated it. He was well aware that the renewal of the sacrifice of Christ was the source of the graces of conversion. He emphasized also Communion, inviting those who were properly prepared to receive Communion more frequently, contrary to the pastoral praxis of the time. You know, again, that the Real Presence of Christ in the Eucharist fascinated him, in the Mass and outside it. He was found so often before the tabernacle in adoration! His poor parishioners in turn were not slow to come and greet Christ and adore him in his Blessed Sacrament. The Council has happily allowed us to renew our eucharistic celebrations, to open them to a participation of the

community, to make them living and expressive. I think that the Cure d'Ars would have been happy at this. Yet we see that, despite this, not everything has progressed. The notable diminution of religious practice, due to multiple causes that I do not wish to analyze here, is a fact that causes great concern. Our faithful must learn again its capital importance in the life of the Christian. This was an essential catechesis for the Cure d'Ars. Besides this, the dignity of the celebration and the spirit of recollection are values that have not always been respected. The Cure d'Ars insisted on creating in his church a whole climate of prayer, which was accessible to the people and tended to promote adoration even outside of Mass. Who would not desire to promote this taste for silent prayer in our churches, this sense of the interior life?

One thing more impresses us: the Cure d'Ars worked hard to restore the sense of Sunday, so that mothers of families and servants would be free to come to the eucharistic assembly. I encourage you to continue to promote the Christian Sunday.

I leave you to meditate on this grace which the Lord gives us, of forgiving sins in his name and of offering his Body in nourishment to our brothers and sister. "A savior with Christ!"

Prayer

Lord Jesus Christ, who gave your life so that all might be saved and have life in abundance, keep alive in us the desire for the salvation of all whom you entrust to our ministry. Renew our readiness to offer them reconciliation with God and with their brethren, like Saint Paul and Saint Jean Marie

Vianney.

We thank you for your Body and Blood, which you permit us to offer each day for the salvation of the world, to receive within ourselves to give to our brothers and sister, and to venerate in our churches. Do not permit our hearts to become accustomed to this gift; let us, like the Cure d'Ars, discern in it your love that goes to the ultimate lengths. You who reign with the Father and the Holy Spirit for ever and ever.

THE THIRD MEDITATION

8. *"We carry this treasure in earthen vessels, so that this extraordinary power may be from God, and may not come from ourselves"* (2 Cor 4:7)

Dear brothers, we had to begin first by meditating on the splendor of the priesthood, on the "extraordinary power" of salvation that God entrusts to us. Yet how could we be un aware of the tribulations of the ministry, which Saint Paul himself experienced? How could we fail to recognize the weaknesses of our "earthen vessels"? I should like to help you to live then in hope and to encourage your efforts to find the sources of help. The Cure d'Ars said, " Do not be afraid of your burden. Our Lord carries it with you."

The difficulties of the apostle can come from outside, when he is faithful in serving Jesus Christ alone. He suffers mockeries and calumny, and his freedom is shackled; as Saint Paul says, he may even be *"harassed on every side"*, *"persecuted"*, *"brought low"*. In some countries, very many priests and Christians suffer these persecutions in silence. Often they have the effect of stimulating and purifying the faith of the faithful. But what a trial! And what an obstacle to the ministry! Let us remain in solidarity with these brothers in their trials.

In the countries of the West, there are other difficulties. You encounter a widespread spirit of criticism, of bad faith, of secularization, even of atheism, or simply of exclusive concentration on material concerns; the message that you wish to bring in the name of Christ and of the Church is relativized or rejected. In the fifties Cardinal Suhard well described the sign of contradiction constituted by the priest in a society that fears his message (see *Le pretre dans la cite*) and classes him among those who belong to the past, or among the utopians. Since then, in many dioceses, the priests have become fewer and the average age has grown higher. This pyramid of ages sometimes makes the integration of the young priests difficult.

The discouragement can even find nourishment in our mentalities as priests. Some may let themselves be conquered by gloominess, by bitterness in the face of failures, or by endless discussions; sometimes there is a hardening of heart that comes from ideologies foreign to the Christian and priestly spirit; sometimes there is even a spirit of systematic distrust with regard to Rome. All of this has weighed and continues to weigh on the dynamism of priests. I have the impression that the young priests are more free vis-a-vis such mentalities. I encourage them, and I invite them also to appreciate the preceding generations of priests who we put to the test but remained faithful; they have borne the burden of the day the heat, in the midst of many changes, and they have carried out their charge very often in the spirit of the gospel.

Finally, each of you knows his own difficulties: of health, of solitude, of family worries, and also the temptations of the world that enter into you; sometimes there is the sentiment of a great spiritual poverty or even humiliating weaknesses. We offer to God this fragility of our "earthen vessels".

It is good for us to know that the Cure d'Ars too knew many trials: the miseries of his body, which was ill treated by the efforts of his ministry and by his fasts, the misunderstanding and calumnies of his parishioners, the critical suspicions and jealousies of his confreres, and more mysterious spiritual trials: what Father Monnin called a certain "supernatural melancholy", spiritual desolations, anguish about his own salvation, an implacable struggle against the spirit of evil, and a certain darkness. Generous and spiritual souls are rarely exempt from these. Yet, despite his keen sensitivity, the Cure d'Ars was not seen to be discouraged. He resisted these temptations.

9. You too know the way of salvation and the means to refresh your strength.

I would say first of all: s spiritual renewal.

How could we bring a remedy to the spiritual crisis of our time, unless we ourselves grasp the means of a profound and constant union with the Lord, whose servants we are?

In the Cure d'Ars, we have an incomparable guide. He said, "The priest is above all a man of prayer....We need reflection, prayer, union with God."

It was with good reason that our spiritual directors insisted on a time of prayer given each day freely, in the presence of the Lord, in the daily listening to the Word of God, in the praise and intercession we make in the name of the Church through the prayer of the liturgy of the hours, in the manner of celebrating the Eucharist every day, in prayer to Mary. What admiration the Cure d'Ars had for our Lady: "My oldest affection"! What confidence: "It is enough to turn to her, to be heard"!

I think further, or regular periods of retreat, to permit the Spirit of God to penetrate us, to "verify" us, and to help us to discern what is essential in our vocation.

It is obvious that we must integrate into our prayer the daily encounter with human beauty and misery in our ministry; it can nourish our prayer, provided that we refer everything to the Lord, "for his glory".

All our priestly commitments take on a new relief in the light of this spiritual vitality:

Celibacy, the sign of our unlimited availability to Christ and to others.

A real poverty, which is a share in the life of the poor Christ and in the condition of those who are poor, as Father Chevrier showed.

Obedience, which is shown in our service in the Church.

The asceticism necessary to every life, beginning with that of the ministry carried out day by day.

The acceptance of the trials that come, and even voluntary mortifications offered with love for souls: the Cure d'Ars knew by experience the truth of that word of the Lord, "There are demons that are cast out only by fasting and prayer."

But, you will ask, Where is one to find the energy for all this? Certainly, we are not dispensed from the necessity to be men of courage. However, "the yoke is sweet and the burden is light", if our courage relies on the belief and hope that the Lord will not abandon those who have consecrated themselves to him: "God is greater than our heart" (1 Jn 3:20).

And more than this, we shall find joy: the emaciated face of the Cure d'Ars seemed always to smile!

10. *"I have become all things to all men: to the weak I became weak"* (1 Cor 9:22).

The priestly ministry, then, living in a state of union with God, is the daily place of our sanctification.

This is how Jesus prayed to the Father for his apostles: "I do not pray that you should take them out of the world, but that you should guard them from the evil one" (Jn 17:15). The Council recommended to pastors that they should never be strangers to the existence and conditions of life of their flock (see Presbyterorum Ordinis, no. 13). In France, many priests of the generation of the Council, and even earlier, have had this concern to a very high degree. This attitude of welcoming, listening, understanding, and sharing is always necessary, so that evangelization may be carried out in a language that is audible and credible. I say this especially to the new generations of seminarians. Father Chevrier made himself poor with those who were poor. It is necessary to penetrate in the same manner the new mentalities of the milieus that are to be evangelized, rich or poor, cultured or not. It is necessary that the missionary vigor of those older than you be maintained through you in today's world. Yet precisely for this reason, the Council adds that priest shall not forget that they are the dispensers of a life other than earthly life, and that they must not model themselves on the present world, but must issue the challenge of the gospel to it. It is not their task to back up the material or political options of their faithful (even when these are legitimate), so that their ministry may be open to all, and clearly oriented toward the Kingdom of God.

11. The spiritual and apostolic quality of the priests of tomorrow is prepared today, and I cannot omit a mention of this formation.

Dear seminarians, what a joy it is for me to see you all gathered together here! I greet in you the next generation of the clergy of France. Even if you are still the little flock of which the gospel speaks, I am full of hope when I see you. And I count on your joy in consecrating your lives to the Church, so that many other candidates will be encouraged to come forward. I believe that you are ready too to accept the demands of this service.

Many of you enter the seminary at a more mature age than in the past, after experience in work or studies. However, as a recent study shows, it is very often the case that your path to the priesthood began before you were thirteen years old. Accept the conditions of discernment and maturity that are proper to your vocation. If God calls you and if the Church so judges, then do not let yourselves be discouraged by the trials through which you pass. I imagine that you know the innumerable difficulties that the young Jean Marie Vianney encountered before her became a priest: the lack of instruction and of contact with educated people, delay because of the French Revolution, the necessity of working on the farm, the distracting fact of military service, and above all the difficulty of learning Latin, the lack of memory, the hesitations of the authorities in the seminary, the late ordination, in solitude, in an occupied country. Certainly, he benefitted from graces: a Christian climate in his family, the effective and tenacious help of Father Balley of Ecully. Yet his path to the priesthood will encourage all those who know trials in the maturing of their vocation.

Your seminaries must be able to welcome different kinds of sensitivity, in a great mutual respect; generous souls must not be held back by the fear of others, nor must they judge them a priori. The bond with the bishop is fundamental, and the accompaniment by a personal spiritual director and the judgment of a team of educators are the guarantee of the vocation. One does not acquire the priesthood: one is called to it by those who judge you suitable, in the name of the bishop.

My desire is that your seminaries may prepare you as well as possible for the priestly life that has been continually before your eyes today. When I received the bishops of this Eastern Central region in their *ad limina* visit in 1982, I said that you must pursue a profound philosophical reflection that includes the metaphysical level, without remaining in an "impressionistic haze"; theology must be approached in the intellectual, scholarly, and spiritual attitude of the most complete initiation possible into the mystery of salvation; listening to the Word of God must take the first place in your houses; formation in the spiritual life, with adequate meetings and the assiduous reading of the great authors, is obviously indispensable. At the same time, you must have the experience of a fraternal community life and of a deepened liturgical and personal prayer. There is room also for a certain apprenticeship of the ministry: how to know the world of today as it is, how to approach it in a pastoral dialogue that is a dialogue of salvation. On the threshold of the priestly life, you must be open to the diversity of the priestly tasks that are necessary for a diocese, and you must be ready for the task that will be entrusted to you.

Happily, many students today seem to desire these demands of seminary life; they represent also a great responsibility for the directors and professors. I pray that the Lord will help them in this very important service of the Church.

12. You priests likewise have need of intellectual refreshment and of the support of the community.

You understand well the necessity of intellectual work, of a kind of permanent formation that will deepen your theological, pastoral, and spiritual reflection (see the Code of Canon Law, can.279). How impressive it is to note that the Cure d'Ars, despite his harassing days, tried to read each day, choosing one of the four hundred books that remained in his library!

I wish also that a true fraternity may unite you, deeper than all the differences, a fraternity that is sacramental and also exists on the level of feelings. Father Chevrier wished to associate other priests and laity with himself.

The religious priests find support in their confreres. The diocesan priests live in a greater solitude, and I think that the priests of the younger generations will find it hard to live alone like the Cure d'Ars. It is certain that many will find a great support and a stimulus to their reflection and their prayer in the associations of priests. I know that these are regaining vitality in France, and I give them my encouragement.

Certain persons or associations of laity, such as the Word of the Countryside, undertake also to help isolated and poor priests. This is very praiseworthy.

However, what I wish to emphasize is the ever-more-intense collaboration between priests and laity in the ministry. There is a great hope for the apostolate in this, and I would say also a great stimulus for the priest himself, if he knows how to trust the laity in their own initiatives and how to help them to discern what is appropriate and how to preserve his own identity as a priest. Even in this field, the Cure d'Ars knew how to obtain the collaboration of his parishioners and to give them greater responsibility.

13. My reflections this morning concern you closely,

dear deacons, because you are the collaborators of the priestly order. I cannot speak of your task without thinking of the attitude of Jesus on Holy Thursday: he rises from table and washes the feet of his disciples, and, at the moment when he institutes the Eucharist, he indicates the service of others as the royal way. The bishop associates you as permanent deacons with the priests, by means of an ordination that puts you forever at the service of the people of God in a manner that is proper to you (see *Lumen Gentium*, no. 29). The Church counts greatly on you, especially for the proclamation of the Work and for catechesis, for the preparation for the sacraments, for the administering of baptism and giving Holy Communion, for presiding over the prayer of the community in certain circumstances, to ensure other services of the Church, and above all, for bringing the testimony of charity in many sectors of the life of society. I am happy to bless you and to bless your families.

14. At the close of this long meditation, I come back to the missionary aspect of our priesthood. Like a good shepherd, we must go to people where they are. There are many kinds of apostolic approaches for this: the discreet and patient presence in friendly closeness, sharing the conditions of life and sometimes of work too in the world of the workers, in the world of those who work intellectually, or in other milieus when these seem to be cut off from the Church and need the daily and credible dialogue of a priest who is in solidarity with their searching for a world that is more just and more brotherly. In this case, priests are less able to exercise the ordinary ministries of their confreres who are parish priests or chaplains. May they know that they have the esteem of

the Church, inasmuch as their motivation is apostolic and they renew themselves in the spiritual life regularly, and in the cases where this corresponds to a mission received from the bishop. May they always give an authentic testimony to the gospel, considering this a priestly function, a preparation of a more complete evangelization! May their membership of one single presbyterate, with which they shall actively seek to maintain frequent and close links, permit them to keep alive in themselves the responsibility of those entrusted with the mysteries of Christ; and may all priests feel themselves in solidarity with their ministry in the service of spreading the gospel! Besides this, the changes that the gospel must cause in society are normally the work of the Christian laity, linked to the priests.

It remains true that all the pastoral efforts of priests must converge, as in the Cure d'Ars, on the explicit proclamation of the Faith, on the forgiveness of sins, on the Eucharist.

Above all, as Paul VI said to your bishops in 1977, never separate mission and contemplation, mission and worship, mission and Church, as if there were on the one hand some who exercise a missionary activity toward those who are on the margins of the Church and, on the other hand, some who prepare for the sacraments and prayer and build up the institution of the Christian Church. Mission is the work of the whole Church: it is inspired by prayer and draws its strength from holiness.

Mission cannot limit itself to the needs of your own country, however great these may be. It is open to the other Churches, to the universal Church that continues to count on the aid of French priests, following in the path of the marvelous missionary generosity that has been alive for a century and a half. The

French dioceses that pursue this endeavor of solidarity, even in their present poverty, rediscover a missionary dynamism for themselves.

15.   However, I do not want to limit my appeal to France. There are priests and bishops here who have come from more than sixty countries of the world. They feel themselves at home in Ars, where the priesthood has shone out with a special brilliance. The example of Saint Jean Marie Vianney continues to give an impetus to parish priests in the whole world and to all the priests who are involved in the very varied tasks of the apostolate.

From this noble place that contrasts with the previous simplicity of the original village, I give thanks to Jesus Christ for this unheard-of gift of the priesthood, that the Cure d'Ars and that of all the priests of yesterday and today. They prolong the sacred ministry of Jesus Christ throughout the world. In the Christian communities that are like the frontier posts of the mission, they work often in difficult, hidden thankless conditions, for the salvation of souls and for the spiritual renewal of the world, which sometimes honors them and sometimes ignores them, disregards them or persecutes them.

Today, in union with all the bishops of the world, my brothers in the episcopate, whose immediate cooperators are the priests, I pay them the homage that they deserve, praying God to sustain them and reward them. I invite all the Christian people to join me in this.

To this word of thanks, I join an urgent appeal to all priests: whatever may be your interior or exterior difficulties, which the merciful Lord knows, remain faithful to your sublime vocation, to the various priestly commitments that make you men wholly available for the service of the gospel. In critical times, remember that no temptation to abandonment is fatal before the Lord who has called you, and know that you can count on the support of your confreres in the priesthood and of your bishops.

The only decisive question that Jesus puts to each one of us, to each pastor, is the one he put to Peter: "Do you love me, do you love me truly?" (see Jn 21:15).

So, dear brothers, have no fear. If the Lord has called us to work in his field, he is with us through his Spirit. Let us be drawn onward by the Holy Spirit, in the Church.

To each of you, seminarians, priests, and deacons and to all those whom you represent, I given my affectionate Apostolic Blessing.

Now we are going to pray to Mary in the Angelus. The Cure d'Ars consecrated this parish to Mary conceived without sin. May she help us to cooperate in the best way possible in the mission of her Son, the Savior!